Identities

YABOME GILPIN-JACKSON

ISBN: 1540657116
ISBN-13: 978-1540657114

DEDICATION

Dedicated to those who identify as African, on and off the continent...

Those who continue to negotiate their identities everyday…

Let's tell our stories….

"…contemporary Africa has a hybrid cultural character that is the product of local and alien mentalities and lifestyles living together in the same communities and individuals. The cultural braid this duality engenders is, theoretically speaking, a more complex lived reality than has hitherto been articulated." A. Bame Nsamenang[1]

---

[1] Nsamenang, A. B. (2003). Conceptualizing human development and education in Sub-Saharan Africa at the interface of indigenous and exogenous influences. In T. S. Saraswathi (Ed.), *Cross-cultural perspectives in human development: Theory, research and applications.* New Delhi, India: SAGE Publications.

CONTENTS

ACKNOWLEDGMENTS

Thank you to my incredible Mother, Haja Fatmatta Kanu, author in her own right, who relentless encouraged me to complete this project. Thank you for reading the manuscript, being my historical fact-checker and Editor-in-Chief. To my mother-in-law Ayodele Gilpin-Jackson, thank you for also reading my early drafts, correcting facts and for all your prayers, love and encouragement.

Thank you to all my siblings. You encourage me all the time in big and small ways. I especially acknowledge you Memuna Williams for telling me I'm awesome, asking me not to take this work for granted and inspiring me to continue writing. Musu Taylor-Lewis, my sister, partner-in-dreaming and neighbor. Thank you for all that, and for reading the manuscript and always spotting my weird writing idiosyncrasies. My friend, my Kenyan sister, Evaline Njoki Lesinko – thank you for saying yes to being my final reader and editor. I will cherish always the image of you on that quiet nursing night shift, editing this book into the wee hours.

To my husband, Adelana Gilpin-Jackson. There are no words. You help me live without limits. We've come a long way and seen many of our dreams come true. We'll travel a long way together yet. I love you. Thank you for letting me bring my laptop to bed many a night to write these stories and for your final impromptu proofreading.

And to my children, Kayla, Jaaziah and Perez. Thank you for letting me write in the middle of our playtimes. Kayla, thank you for noticing I love stories and for all your curiosity about what I write and why. My heart soared the day you said: "Mummy you are always writing stories, I'm going to work on my book too." I hope you do. I pray this book helps you remember you must always tell your stories.

1 WHERE ARE YOU FROM?

Today, like every other day, I get up and prepare for an ordinary day. I wake to the sound of my deliberately annoying alarm tunes. It's a soukous track called *Diblo Dibala*, which actually means Good Morning. I would normally be pulsating to it on a dance floor, with my Congolese friends who'd introduced it to me, but at 6am in the morning, it only makes me cringe. I swear to myself again that I will change it before bed tonight. I wonder as I brush my teeth why I never do. I stare at myself in the mirror, eyeing my wild 'fro. It is tightly coiled, matted on the left side into a grove where my pillow had nestled my head all night. The right side looked like a pile of soft black wool twisted into any and every shape. It is always matted, my left side, because I refuse to face the right and stare at the empty expanse of the ocean of my bed. It is how I cope while I wait for God to send me Mr. Right. I face the window on the right so I can look at the night sky and dream.

The night sky always calms me. When I stare at the dark expanse with its twinkling lights I feel myself being transported to the land of my birth. I imagine the sounds of night that I don't hear in the night here. Things are quiet here, too quiet, other than the occasional car driving by. So I imagine the sounds of people talking in loud excited bursts. Talking to each other and over each other.

Horns blaring, a radio loudly heralding BBC Africa headlines in sound competition and confusion with the corner store guy's Afrobeat playlist. It is the same playlist every night, continuing like a broken record until you are in a love and hate relationship with the music. You can tell which neighbor loves it by the direction of the "turn off the music!!" shriek, followed by the laughter of those who are still in love for the moment. Tomorrow they trade roles. Those sounds, a raucous melody I'd never have expected to miss.

I finish brushing my teeth and start on my hair. I generously spray it with my mixture of water and conditioner, my basic miracle serum as I call it. Then I don a shower cap to further soften it in the steam of the shower. I remember my surprise when I realized that's all I needed to soften my hair enough for an afro comb to go through it, as long as my scalp and roots were already well moisturized with an oil-based hair grease. That was the day I had a purging ritual for all my natural hair products – piles of hair creams, moisturizers and sprays, all promising to unravel my natural curls – none remotely resulting in the perfectly coiffed head of loose to tight but all well-defined ringlets on the packages. All they did for me was shrink my hair into an un-combable mess. It felt freeing to release the dream of perfect curls down the garbage chute.

Nowadays, after a wash, deep conditioner and light blow-dry, I part my hair straight down from the middle of my forehead to the middle of the nape of my neck, then part each half into another half, forming four equal rows. I carefully work from the bottom to the top of each section, parting and liberally applying hair grease to the scalp and massaging it through. Then I plait each row into a cornrow or French braid from the top back down, sealing the moisture and oils in. On nights that I do my plaits, I unravel them in the morning, then finger comb or brush my hair into some shape. A full fro today, a fro-hawk tomorrow, whatever my fingers feel like creating. On nights that I was too tired like last night, I'd sleep as-is with no plaits, knowing that I would wake up with the groove on my left side but my well-oiled hair would be forgiving under the spray of my basic serum. This, was the same hair ritual that generations of women in my lineage had done to tend their hair. I remember my grandma doing this regularly and reminding me to "fold my hair into plaits" when it started looking too matted or wild in grade school. I'm still baffled as to why I had given up this ritual, in the quest for perfectly chemically straightened hair in high school and then for the promise of easy-coiffed curls in a bottle.

Forty-five minutes later, I am ready. Today, I had done a diagonal part from one side of my head down to the opposite back-side, then done a French braid with a bit of hair extension around the outside edges of both sides and tucked in the length of the braid into a loose bun in the back. I wore a bright orange blouse and grey pantsuit with a pair of string beads and small stud earrings that were a curious blend of pink pearl, tan and orange hues. I wolfed down my peanut butter toast and poured my tea into my travel mug while I packed my lunch sandwich. I was trying to pack lunches instead of buying to save a bit of money – funny how that adds up to something. My cousin who called here the land of milk and honey needed help again and I'd promised to send her money this month. I knew she often swindled me for extra cash, but I didn't mind. She took care of Ma's needs and always got everything I needed done properly and on time. That is rare across the oceans these days.

I am just in time to make the 5-minute walk to the bus that takes me to the train station. I slip into my tan pumps. By that I mean my dark brown shoes that match my dark brown shiny skin. I check myself out in the full-length mirror by the door. I like the reflection staring back at me. I'd come to terms long time ago with being average. Average height, average build, average looks, not striking in any way. I do wish I looked more like the Nollywood actress Genevieve Nanji, but oh well.

I'm ready for the walk to the bus station – I call it the zombie walk. Human beings walking beside each other, silently. This one still waking up, that one on their smart device, the other clearly late and rushing by. Me, focused on sipping my hot tea to keep warm in the chilly morning air. I used to relish this walk. It was the most definable way I could describe freedom and independence. The sensation of feeling grown up as you lock your front door and make your way to a job where you work to pay your own bills, with no obligation to greet anyone along the way. I also used to love riding the bus. In my early working days after finishing my degree, I could not get over the irony that in this place, the well-off ride the bus and train too. It seemed to me this was a place where people forgo everyday comforts, yet indulge in exorbitant pleasures – food and drink like caviar and fine wines - that would supply a whole household's meal in other parts of the world.

Nowadays, the novelty has worn off. I spend the zombie walk wondering what is truly happening to people in their lives. On other days, I'm too enmeshed in thoughts of my own life to notice someone who could use a smile. I sigh as I transfer from the bus to the subway. I catch the gaze of the Chinese-looking girl as I climb into the train car. She smiles at me. I returned a tight distracted smile as my subconscious registers that she sometimes rides the bus with me. I thought vaguely how much life feels bland right now. Ritualistic and rote. I need some spice and color. My bright shirt feels like the only spark in my life right now.

I get off at my usual stop and another brisk 5-minute walk later, I am walking through the glass double doors of my office building. By now, I have warmed up and the tea in my mug is tepid. I really need to buy a new travel mug. I get into the elevator before the doors close. There were only three of us in there. The three of us pretend not to look relieved that the doors close just as the next throng of people coming into the building come into view. We punch in our floor numbers. The girl on my left was the first off on the 10th floor, I am on the 13th floor and the man on my right punches in for the 17th floor. We settle in for the ride, with a brief nod of acknowledgement to absolve ourselves of our disconnected humanity. Appeased, we stare straight ahead, as if we couldn't wait to be free of the confines of being in the same space for the two-minute ride.

As soon as the elevator starts its ascent, I hear the voice on my right say:

"Where are you from?"

I feel the warmth rising from my stomach as I go into an amygdala hijack. I stare even more stoically ahead in the hope that the voice isn't directed at me, even though my heart already knows the answer. The voice floats again through the veil of the battling emotions assailing me.

"Where are you from?"

I feel my body turn to the left and hear my voice saying:

"Do you get asked that randomly in elevators?!"

I watch the girl's cheeks flush bright red and her lips open to form a response. The elevator rumbles to a stop and I feel her flood of relief as she looks apologetically at me and bolts off on 10.

I feel trapped and consider bolting off the elevator with her but my rational brain is still in shock and isn't moving as fast as I want it to. What was I supposed to do now? I turned to the right and said with a cynical smile:

"Why do you ask?"

My interrogator looks suddenly shifty and mumbles: "just curious I guess…" flipping open his commuter magazine and burying his face in it.

Before I could collect myself to say anything else, the doors open for me. I say pointedly:

"Have a great day" and sashay off. I suddenly feel defiantly confident, saying with my walk: *I belong here.*

I still can't understand how my relationship to the question: Where are you from has changed so drastically over the years. Fifteen years ago, when I newly arrived to accept my undergraduate university scholarship, I was amused by the question. It seemed so novel and yet so out of place to be randomly asked that question. I used to wonder why so many people here seemed to know precious little about anywhere else. It was either that or the confident alternative:

"I heard you're from Angola – isn't it terrible what happened there. You must be so happy to be here."

It was like there was no in between, no space for alternatives, no grey area. Like I never existed apart from what happened there. Only black and white. The visible and invisible me. Seen and unseen. So, I started out patiently explaining who I was, where I came from and how I was much more than the veiled assumptions in the questions with which I was placed in a box, over and over again. I explained my hair. I told others that my family had lived in Ghana, where English was the official and instructional language at the colonial-established universities and that it was normal for students like me to get full scholarships abroad from there. I shared that I did eat regular meals three times a day although yes, it is true that food security and armed conflict was an issue in some countries on the continent. That I did not live with wildlife everywhere around me. I had to explain many a time why I spoke Portuguese, English and French because in addition to Portuguese from Angola, my family also lived in Togo, which is French and where I did middle school on our move to British West Africa.

Over time, my amusement gave way to irritation, then all out anger as the box became too suffocating to bear. I'd erupt like a volcano at this commonplace interrogation, stung by the fact that I'd be the only one at the dinner party to be asked the question by the friend of a mutual acquaintance who would have just met me for all of two minutes. More recently, my anger had given way to indifference. I simply chose when to engage and when not to. Sometimes giving an uninformative response like "from here," or "from this planet," or "from everywhere!" or "It's a long story." Other times, I'd give into the torrent of insidious curiosity with which I am deemed exotic. I would mutter a defeated "Africa" or "Angola" even as my heart would pound at me for the betrayal of stepping into the box so easily.

I've been surprised a couple of times to realize that not all the curiosity is uninformed, just maybe misplaced. Like the one time this lady made a bee-line for me.

"Hi," she said.

"Hi," I responded.

"Where are you from?" she queried.

At the time, I was at the place between being amused and taken aback by the question. I eyed the lady intently. She was older, with a kind face and open smile. She had short dark hair and brown skin. She looked South Asian and spoke with a crisp British accent. It occurred to me that while I had been curious about her, I hadn't thought it appropriate to ask about her background devoid of any connection with her. Finally, assuming she wouldn't know where Angola was anyway, I answered, "Africa."

She retorted: "I know you are from Africa, but where, what country?!"

In the exchange that followed, I learnt she had met and married someone from neighboring Namibia and lived there for years. She introduced me to her daughter and I introduced her to my mother and concurrent friendships began. I love that story and those two are still like family to me. I often wonder what would have happened if she had never approached me.

I try to collect myself as I turn around the corner to my desk. Karen the too-bubbly analyst on our floor is bobbing out of the lunchroom and sing-songs out to me:

"Oh, hey there Miss Thang! Oh, nice hair today, girl – How do you get it like that?!"

I stop in my tracks, steady myself and say to her: "Good morning to you too Karen!"

"Good morning! But seriously, how do you get your hair like that – it's always so different"

I can't help smiling. She's relentlessly happy this one. She at least knows me well enough to ask about my hair.

"It's a long story Karen. And I have to get to my desk"

"Fine" she answers – "let's do lunch then. You're always evading my lunch requests. If you're not dieting, you're not eating out coz you are saving money. Or..."

"Fine!" I interrupt her to say "I'll come for lunch today." I think of the sandwich in my bag and decide I'll have it with a salad for dinner.

The rest of the day flies by. Lunch with Karen is a whirlwind. She was used to the idea of my hair by then and forgot to ask. I didn't remind her. At the end of the day I join the weary zombies walking back home. I run into the girl from the elevator in the morning. She avoids catching my eyes. I start walking. The next time I am conscious, I am getting off the train and back on the bus ride to my street. The Chinese-looking girl is smiling at me. I smile back, then quickly take my novel out of my purse to signal I am not in the mood to talk. I'm reading Taiye Selasi's *Ghana Must Go.* The girl keeps smiling at me every time I look up to check what stop we've reached. Two more stops later, I am getting out when I realize my smiling co-passenger is alighting right behind me.

"Hi. Where are you from?"

A wave of exhaustion and resignation washes over me. I look at her, manage a weak smile and say:

"Angola."

"Oh awesome! I knew you were from somewhere in Africa! I'm from Mauritius!"

"Oh!" I manage. Stunned by the realization I had not even remotely considered the possibility.

She waves as she runs off to the car that is waiting to pick her at the bus stop. "I'll see you tomorrow! Let's sit together okay."

Back home, I kick off my shoes at the door. It was a quiet evening ahead for me. No planned movie dates with girlfriends. No Mr. Right on the horizon. My cousin calls to ask when I'll send the money. She tells me: "Use MoneyGram eh, the rates are way better than Western Union."

I want to talk to Ma, but she gets on the phone only long enough to say she is off to an engagement ceremony:

"I'm waiting for your engagement eh!" She says. "You will meet someone soon by God's Grace! If not, you must come home and meet someone here! I can introduce you to our old neighbor's son, Shuma. He returned home two years ago, and he's still single!" I happily let her hurry off the phone.

After tidying up, I eat my sandwich and salad and settle in front of the TV. The assault of terrorism reports that greeted me when I turned it on made my stomach flip over. I am not in the mood to swallow that reality today. I switch it off and continue reading *Ghana Must Go.* By 10 pm, I am yawning. I make my way to my bed. No hair ritual tonight, I'll leave my slanted French braids in for tomorrow. I lay down on my left side. I pray. Then close my eyes and am transported to an Angolan sunset night. Tonight, we all love the Afrobeat. It's the Nigeria duo PSquare singing *Personally.* All the neighbors are happy and dancing. As I dance and drift off, a handsome Mr. Right appears. He smiles as he approaches me, puts out his hand and said: "Hi, I'm Silo. I'm from Zambia. You interested in going for coffee? I'd like to know more about you."

2 TOO MUCH WATER IN THE GARRI

John was incensed. To look at him you wouldn't know it. He sat with his perfect parker pen, in his perfectly tailored suit, in the board room of the accounting firm where he worked. He was pretending to take notes on the financial documents of the organization audit they were discussing, but he couldn't detach himself from the phone conversation with his sister River a few minutes before. Not even the brilliant colors of the shedding fall trees and the stunning mountain view of the Vancouver skyline outside the glass windows could placate him. That view was usually his solace from the boredom and drudgery of talking numbers in this boardroom, in this job he was in only to please his parents. Today, the view didn't give him an escape. It fueled the anger churning in him.

"What's up River?" He'd said as he finished the last bite of his lunch. He'd grabbed his files as he looked at his watch. It was 12:56pm.

"I'm in a meeting in 4 minutes, so make this quick."

River had retorted: "*And as always, I love that you picked up my call in spite of that, Mr. Big Shot.*"
She'd paused. An intentional break in the space between her ear and his that had him instinctively sit up.

"How come you didn't pick up Mom's calls? And Dad's? All morning?"

"Oh, come on, you know the answer, sis. I don't have time for their long-winded stories when I'm trying to prepare for a critical board meeting! Of what else they are doing to enjoy their hard-earned money and latter days. Of how proud they are of us for not letting them down. Oh…and of the newest expectation, the next thing or next adventure we must go on to continue our service to them and to humanity. To honor the sacrifices they'd made so we could be…"

"Too late for that." She'd said, interrupting his high-pitched mimicry with a chuckle in her voice. "*Our two-week family vacation for thanksgiving is no longer at Whistler, buddy. Nope, we are off to Africa. The parents are already in London. I'm picking you up at the office at 6pm.*"

"What the…!" John all but screamed. And click went the phone.

The buzz of the dial tone after the severed connection matched the building buzz in his ear, in his brain and the heat in his heart. He slammed the blackberry down and clung to the side of the desk for a moment. He hated this. Hated being bossed around and told what to do. He hated being controlled and manipulated into subordinating to his parents' wishes time and again. And yet, as sure as morning would come, he knew he would be on that flight with River. He hated himself for not being able to stand up to them and say no.

~~~

John had tried saying no to his dad before. It was the last days of junior high school and the campus was alive with the buzz and talk of plans for senior high. This was crucial you see, because history had shown that the move to senior school was the beginning and the end of many things in the elite private school he and River had attended, the best in the province. The high school specialized in Academics and the Arts. The promise was that your child would have entry into the best universities and programs thereafter. There were only a few shared courses on the curriculum once the high school selections were made, as even the buildings that housed the state of the art facilities in either area were separated. In general, it was the end of the collective experience at Saint Peters as the nerds got separated
~~~

from the cool kids. It was also the beginning of many anticipated romances, culminating with graduation dance proposals and partnerships. John and his squad had spent the last six months of junior school in feverish dialogue about their futures. As a result, he was as certain of three things as he was that his image would stare back at him when he stood in front of a mirror. First, his talent and his desired future lay in the Arts. Second, he was in love with Carly and had vowed to marry her. Third, his father would never approve of the first and the second.

You see, in his dad's world, only an academic and a professional path to success mattered. He had clawed his way to success in a construction job and was reminded of that every time the fingers on his left hand caused him pain from the cold when summer turned to fall and fall into winter. The pain was from a workplace accident that had resulted in his hand being crushed between a wall and some heavy machinery at a demolition site he'd been working on. John could still remember the -40 degrees Celsius Edmonton night, when his dad's screams sliced the freezing air over and over again, because he could find no relief from the chronic pain.

They'd run out of every painkiller in the house and to venture to the 24-hour corner store was out of the question. River was 2 then, and wouldn't stop crying because of the screams. His mom had moved gallantly between Dad and River trying to calm them down, all while the wind howled on. John was 5 and had cowered on his bed, covering his head with a pillow to drown it all out. He'd been trying to help Mom by not crying also. He had fallen asleep at some point. When he woke up, he'd wet his bed. Within a month, they'd packed up and were headed to Beautiful British Columbia, where a sub-zero or snowy winter day was a novelty that had children run out to capture the moment and play with their snowy guest, because by morning the rain might have also visited and washed it all away.

John's dad had already determined before the move that he wanted more for his family and wouldn't afford it working construction. He worked all day and would pour over books while John's mom worked cleaning offices overnight to make ends meet. John remembers one of his dad's crew stumbling across one of the books one day. John had noticed his dad carefully tuck the book away under the couch before the guys came over for drinks. At some point that night, one of them dropped a pen and moved the couch to get it. Next thing John heard was:

"What the fuck are you reading Construction Management for Dummies for?!"

Another guy retorted: *"It's the last part, cause he's a dummy, dummy!"* There was raucous laughter.

John's dad threw a quick retort back: *"Just you wait till I'm your boss fellas!"* and joined the laughter.

That night, John saw his dad lay his head on top of the book looking worn and tired. He'd gone over and placed his small hand on his dad's wide shoulders:
"You're not a dummy, Daddy, you're the boss!"

Dad had squeezed him tight and said:
"Don't worry son, you will never have to go through this, you will never be humiliated because you can't afford a better lifestyle. You will go to the best schools and learn how to make real money very fast. I'll make sure of it!"

John's dad applied for a construction management position as soon as they moved to Vancouver and landed a job. A month later, one of the crew members from Edmonton called. He was the only guy who hadn't laughed at the *Construction Management for Dummies* joke:

"Hey man, do you still want to be the boss? Wanna pitch in with me to buy a unit in the new high-rise we are working on?"

The two struck a deal and approached the developers to buy a unit. They offered ideas for making the project better, and the developers were impressed with their ideas. The developers were also in the midst of construction union and crew challenges. They offered John and his partner a consulting fee to be their strategizers and negotiators with the crew. Next came a small share offer for development improvements. Dad seized every opportunity. Soon, one unit became two and then several. He sent John and River to

Saint Peters where their mom connected with the working moms and started doing home organizing jobs for them. Her keen eye for design and ability to tailor everything from cushion covers to clothing and source out unique antiques from around the world quickly earned her a referral reputation and high rates. They were on the move. Dad and Mom never let John and River forget their humble beginnings and always told them how they would start in a ***real*** office and how they were to marry well. Their parents were clear that marrying well meant into a family that already had it made and were not struggling. His lady love Carly was the only other kid from a working-class background, and worse, she was from a single-family home. Her mom was a teacher's assistant by day and a cleaner by night. That's how John knew his dad would say no to him becoming a non-income-generating artist and marrying Carly.

His friends convinced him otherwise though. He was becoming a man, they said. Off to high school where they made their own decisions. The dummies told him to ask for what he wanted. After all, his group of 5 friends were all going into the Arts, and choosing a different path by heading to nerdville would be social suicide. The more they said he should, the more he believed them. So, on that spring morning, when John got off the school bus, he was ready. He walked in all pumped up with his budding manhood and bolted into Dad's office.

"*Ah John, just the man I wanted to see! I met Principle Blake for lunch today. I handed him our annual donation to the school and we selected your courses. You are all registered for Academics. You'll be working on a mix of hard sciences, social sciences and business courses this first year so we can really get a sense of your strengths and direction for university. He mentioned your teachers say you are quite talented, perhaps even a gifted artist. I told him you've chosen to take that up as a hobby. I bought you a new easel on the way home.*"

John heard himself say in a squeezed distant voice: "*Dad! I actually want to choose the Arts not Academics!*"

His dad's eyes pierced through him from above the glasses perched on his nose. *"What did you say, son?"*
His dad looked a far cry from the tired, worn construction worker

with his defeated head on *Construction Management for Dummies*. He looked, strong, assured and confident, wearing the air of new wealth. *"Nothing Dad, nothing..."* John mumbled. *"Thank you for the easel."*

John never touched the easel. It was a symbol of his lost dreams. His best friend Travis married Carly. He was the best man. He could forgive his dad for destroying his hopes of marrying Carly. He told himself she didn't look so hot after his godson was born anyway. He couldn't forgive his dad for destroying his first love of the Arts though. He was reminded of that every day in his mind-numbing accounting job with the picturesque window view that he mentally painted and repainted daily.

~~~

"I hate these pilgrimages! Why do I have to go on these freaking trips? Honestly, if I were an immigration minister I would present legislative changes so no visas would be given to any Africans anyway."

John was ranting. River had picked him up and announced she was chaperoning him to his apartment to pack a suitcase and head straight to the airport. He admired River. She was the steady one. When she walked, her strides oozed with the confidence with which she carried herself and that made her beautiful. She also had an eclectic edgy sense of style, imbued with fashion yet a uniqueness that only she could pull off. John was used to heads turning when he walked with his sister.
"That is precisely why you are not the immigration minister, buster!" She said as they entered the elevator.

John glared. River flashed her winning smile back. They had company in the elevator so John held it together long enough for the doors to open on the 15th floor. They were barely out when he blurted:

"I mean, take Emeka or whatever his name is down the hall and his group of shady friends – the guy is a loser! He does nothing but smoke and womanize all day – wanna guess where he gets his money from to live here and keep up his lifestyle! 419 if you ask me!"
~~~

"That's why no one is asking you and keep it down with your crazy talk already!' River retorted.

"You know better than that - How about Dami, the dentist who lives on the 10th floor. Or your friend Shola the lawyer? They are losers too and shouldn't be allowed into the country either? Get packing! Remember it's 35 degrees over there. We don't have a lot of time and I need to call the parents and tell them we are all set."

"Don't you dare put me on the phone! I can't handle that right now!" John screamed.

River grinned: 'Don't worry, I'll tell them you are shitting! All over the place that is!" He threw a pillow at her.

An hour later after a frenzy of packing they were on the way. He had heard from River's monologue that their parents had headed on to arrange entry visas for them on the other side and would meet them at the airport. He'd heard them asking how he was and wanting to talk to him. River had smiled sweetly at him as she said: *"Oh, he is fine, but in the bathroom right now. He seems to have a touch of diarrhea."* She'd quickly lowered her cellphone and said: *"of the mouth that is!"* and then back on the phone: *"What's that mom? Imodium? Yes, we'll get some. We definitely want to make sure he's not runny when we get there!"*

John's mouth was still running at the airport. As they headed to the security line-up, River tucked her arm underneath his and said:

"Come on! What can be soooo terrible about a trip to Africa! Think of it as one of those world adventure make-believe games we used to play when we were kids. Remember when we were pretending to be African monkeys and mom and dad lost it because we were being silly and noisy instead of in bed!"

They started laughing hysterically at the memory. John could feel the wave of rage in him subside, flowing from high to low tide. He knew it was because he was with River. Being with her always brought him sanity and sometimes brought out the worse in him, because with River he could stop pretending to have it all together. When they had finally almost composed themselves, John looked at her and said between giggles in his baritone, laced with the sulky undertone of the hurt 14-year old boy trapped within him:

"You see River, that's it exactly – we aren't kids anymore, but we keep following their rules. We keep saying sorry and climbing quietly into bed. I don't want to see African monkeys running around or starving World Vision kids or drive in dusty off-roading conditions all day in the middle of city streets!"

"REALLY*!!!'* It took John a moment to realize the incredulous voice didn't belong to River. They both spun around and watched as the owner of the voice simultaneously rolled her eyes, hissed through her teeth and stalked off muttering: "These ignorant, ignorant fatted calves!" River collapsed into hysterics again.

When they boarded their flight to London, John and River were sitting across an aisle from each other. That was the best they could do given their late booking and John always wanted aisle seats to help the discomfort of his long legs when they were occasionally in economy. As they plunked down into their seats, John realized he was sitting next to "Hissy Girl" from the security line-up, as they had baptized her. He spun around to plead River into taking his seat. River was sitting low, her face partially covered with *I am Malala* which she had just purchased for flight reading. Her shoulders were bobbing and a tear was rolling down her cheeks as she shook with laughter. John was trapped on a very full long-haul flight that had just gotten longer.

~~~

He was trapped. Stuck in a building with a bulldozer approaching. His hand had just been crushed and he was going to be crushed again. Suddenly a silverback African gorilla approached, picked up the bulldozer and threw it aside. Terror rose in him as the gorilla beat its chest. He very lucidly thought: *Aren't silverback gorillas from Congo?* John woke up, disorientated and in a sweat as they landed in Lungi airport, Sierra Leone, West Africa.
~~~

The journey was a blur. The leg to London was long. Hissy girl blatantly ignored him and River fell asleep with *I am Malala* on her chest. He'd been listless and barely slept the whole flight. They didn't have much time at Heathrow and had to race through the airport to board their connecting flight to Sierra Leone in time. The flight was packed. John was stunned by the change in demographics compared to the flight from Vancouver. He'd been thankful to be in business class this time. He had a splitting headache that was getting worse with the high-pitched concoction of excited voices all around him. He couldn't tell whether people were talking, arguing or just excited as they shoved too full and too large cabin bags into the overhead bins. The overhead bins looked like colic stomachs that were still relentlessly being stuffed with Ghana Must Go bags like candy. The loudness irritated and embarrassed him. As he'd settled in to sleep, Hissy Girl had walked past, headed to economy and whispered a sarcastic: *"have a good rest!"* He'd thrown his hands up and thought -- *Just my luck! Of course she'd be the one going all the way to Freetown with us from Vancouver!*

Now, he was groggy as they disembarked. He was also unprepared for the heat wave that hit him at the top of the flight stairs, as well as the smell of dust, and the canvas of contradictions that greeted him. Although he would later see beggar children, it was not them but stern, professional black African men and women who ushered him into the airport shuttle waiting to take them to the terminal. The road was riddled with potholes but there was a building before him, not a shack for the terminal. There were no monkeys in sight. The blue sky and the brilliant hues of the setting sun marked an incomprehensible portrait on the skyline mixed with tin shacks and concrete buildings. As he took it all in, he suddenly realized the weight of his privileged, sheltered life and he heard hissy girl's voice say *"ignorant fatted calf."* An unusual excitement also rose up within him. This place, right here, was the canvas he'd been waiting for.

John collapsed onto the bench in the shuttle, his face registering the culture shock starting to rock through him. Hissy girl climbed in after him, and offered a tentative, knowing smile, looking sympathetic. When the shuttle stopped, she slipped him a piece of paper with a number and whispered: "call me if you want to talk about it."

"Aunty Carole - Kushe kushe – we gladie for see you oh!' *Greetings Aunty Carole, we are happy to see you.*

"Una sef kushe ya – Tenke, ar gladie for cam back." *Greetings to you too. Thank you, I'm glad to be back.*

He watched in amazement as Hissy Girl, bantered in the local pidgin English, Krio, with the drivers and then with the flood of porter boys who swarmed the shuttle as they got off.

Through the fog of his mind, he recognized the handwriting on the sign that read:

John AND River.

It was his dad's handwriting. Another flood of recognition swept over him as a woman walked by, tall and regal, exuding the same air River always had, of being confident in her own skin. Skin that was as olive brown as that of the woman who just walked by and as his own.
"Sewa!" John shouted towards River above the noise to get her attention.
He was shocked to hear himself call her Sewa and not River. She was still talking to Mark, an acquaintance from Saint Peters they had recognized as they disembarked. On hearing John, she started to say goodbye.

"Sewa?" Mark echoed in just as surprised a tone as John's.
"Yeah, I'm named after the River Sewa here in Sierra Leone – that's my first and middle name. I went by Sewa when I was younger. It's like you and using Mark instead of Mahmoud."

She'd just found that out about him. Mahmoud was Lebanese-Sierra Leonean. He'd sheepishly also confessed he knew they were of Sierra Leonean descent because he'd heard their parents speak Krio once. He said he hadn't said anything because he didn't want to explain his African roots at school. River had smiled at him, thinking of her parents as she'd said: "*how far did that get you?!*" Now River continued:

"Sewa was too interesting, too different…too unfamiliar. I got tired of my friend's parents in kindergarten saying what an 'interesting unique' name I had, followed by 'do you know where it is from, dear?'" When I was going to grade 1, I told my parents to register me as River. That was interesting, but not unfamiliar."

"So, is John's name actually Yusufu or something like that then?" Mark asked.

"Nope silly, it's just plain old John – named after Saint John as a matter of fact."

"Sewa!" John's voice rang out above the crowd. Surer, confident now in his switch to her other name. It was befitting here.

"I gatta go. See you around here? And if not, I'll call you when we get back to Vancouver." They smiled at each other, both silently questioning whether striking up a friendship, or something more, was worth it.

Sewa caught up with John. She took in his bewildered look and said:

"Are you ok, buddy?"

He nodded. She followed his gaze to Hissy Girl. She was surrounded by kids jumping up and down and hugging her with shouts of "Aunty Carole! Aunty Carole! Welcome! Kushe! Tenke for cam back!" Carole's blond hair and pale skin stuck out among the children in their shades of chocolate skin, her face smooshed between heads crowned with afros and cornrows and single braids.

"Her name is Carole," he said needlessly.

Ahead of them they could see their parents waving to them. John had never seen his parents look so excited. And so different. It was as if being here, in this place full of beauty and contradictions, in this place where he could already paint a thousand pictures that'll tell a thousand stories, his parents could finally drop all their guards and all their pretenses.

To see John in that moment, you would not recognize the accountant from Vancouver. His shirt was ruffled and damp, sticking to him as sweat poured out of him in the 35-degree heat. He looked like a little boy who was lost and yet excited. He and River closed the distance to their parents in a quick trot.
He heard his dad say:

"Welcome, welcome my children. We are overjoyed you are here. There is good news and bad news. Things are not the same. But as the Sierra Leonean adage goes: "wata don pass garri" -- there's too much water in the garri cereal. It was time for you to come to understand your heritage and to understand us. It was time for us to stop ignoring that this is where we came from."

John felt something break in him and he suddenly felt lighter than he had in years. He instinctively moved in to give his parents a bear hug and to his surprise, tears sprung to his eyes. His mom hugged him back as she hissed:

"Hush now. Men don't cry in public here! Wait till we get home!"

He heard Sewa's distinctive laughter ring out. The journey had just begun.

3 ONCE UPON A TIME AT FOURAH BAY COLLEGE

Fourah Bay College, University of Sierra Leone, Freetown

Circa The 1990s

It is 6pm on Friday night and the campus has suddenly come alive. The energy is palpable. I think of this time of day on campus as the equivalent of the breaking of dawn on a Sierra Leonean morning. Life erupts suddenly at 6pm Friday on campus, just like the morning comes alive with no transition, emerging suddenly from the stillness with cocks crowing, frogs croaking and pots clanging. Admittedly, the buzz of the waking does begin sometime on Wednesday or Thursday evening with one activity or the other. But it really is like the lackluster cloud that hangs over us gets sucked out and replaced - precisely at 6pm on Friday night - with an air of revelous anticipation. The campus is suddenly filled with laughter, the buzz of chatting and loud callouts from every angle as students mill around. Just like right now. Someone just shouted out a phrase from a Bob Marley song:

♪ ♪ *We're jammin', jammin', jammin'!!!* ♪ ♪

And a number of random others just responded equally loudly:

♪ ♪ *I wanna jam it wid you!* ♪ ♪

A taxi pulls up to 'bus tik', the bus loop, transit stop and meeting point where literally every transaction, transportation and otherwise, happens on this campus. At least 15 students all rush forward towards the taxi as the passengers in it simultaneously try to disembark. There's shouting and shoving. A minute later, there are 10 new student passengers stuffed into the 5-seater taxi. I am still amazed at how that happens. The 5 losers are complaining about being shoved aside even though they were front of the pack. The onlookers sitting at what is for all intents and purposes the bus loop waiting area, commonly called, The Stone, laugh heartily at the spectacle of it all. Couples who are openly dating walk along with their arms across each other's shoulders. Knowing licentious looks are exchanged by others who are 'underground couples' to confirm rendezvous for later in the night.

This, was a typical Friday evening at Fourah Bay College - FBC. We were getting ready for a revelry-filled weekend and we could hardly wait.

My name is Sia Lansana. You know that means I am an eldest daughter from the Kono-Kissi tribe. Since I have two sisters, you also know my second sister's name is Kumba and my third, Finda, their names also matching their birth order. We have 2 brothers and just like every other first and second-born Kono sons, their names are Sahr and Tamba. I am the second eldest, born five years after Sahr. Sahr graduated from FBC the year before I started and now lives in London, where he is finishing his law degree. Kumba is at a 6th form boarding school and will join me on campus in a year, a thought that terrifies me. Finda and Tamba who are the youngest are still at home in Kono with our parents. My dad is now the Head of Blue Sky mining, where he's worked and progressed through the ranks since I was a child. My mom still runs our family's bed and breakfast hostel, where most expatriate miners stay on their many trips in and out of Kono. I've lived in Freetown with my dad's sister Aunty Kumba Lansana since secondary school. Aunty Kumba is a babe – stylish and beautiful. She's the kind of Aunty you told almost everything. And she's the exact opposite of my stern father. Living with Aunty Kumba and then attending FBC has been the highlight of my life so far.

I'm going towards bus tick to take the shortcut to the Fullah-guy's corner shop. I'm walking briskly, planning to buy some bread to eat with leftover stew for dinner before we head to tonight's party. It's the WeYone club party tonight. WeYone club is the exclusive club for all the cool guys and gals on campus. It means Our Own Club. I'm not a member, but for some reason, I am friends with most WeYone club members and the fact that I have an invitation to the party tonight makes me cool too. Or almost cool. Almost. That seems to be the story of my life. Just like I'm second born. And a girl, not a boy. And almost beautiful. A fact I am reminded of as my gorgeous roommate Mariama runs up to me yelling:

"Sia, Sia, wait me!" That's Krio, Sierra Leone's lingua franca predominantly spoken in Freetown and across the country by most people. The language developed to communicate across indigenous ethnic groups from the Provinces and the Creole descendants of repatriate and re-captive slaves who returned to the continent to form our historic capital Freetown back in the day.

A grin lights up my face as she reaches me. We embrace mid-stride and keep walking.

"Hey, Roomie. You don ready for dis net" *Are you ready for tonight?*

"Na one go be tiday!" *It's on tonight!*

We hear a cat-call coming our way. We ignore it.

"You don decide wetin for wheer?" *Have you decided what to wear?*

"No oh! You geh for hep me." *No, you have to help me*

We hear the cat-call again. A slow whistle, followed by a deep and pointed: "Ar say sista!" *Hey girl!*

Mariama's beautiful oval eyes flash in irritation. Her high cheekbones seem to get even higher as she puckers her lips to let out the typical Sierra Leonean hiss - a sucking sound from air released between the teeth, called a Suck Teet. Her perfectly proportional nose barely moves as she crinkled her face through the hiss. That nose - the feature in Mariama's face that I envy the most. It is the exact opposite of my broad and flat bridge, with wide nostrils. There is no doubt in my mind that even though I was the stereotypically preferred light-skinned and non-bleached girl - Yalla Gyal - I pale, even fade next to Mariama's dark glowing skin and beauty. The only thing I have on her is 3 inches over her 5ft 2inches. And she makes that up in spunk.

"Ous kine kraise man!..." *What kind of crazy guy...!*

I burst out laughing and shout, "You Sullay!" I give the culprit a hug before Mariama can finish her tirade.

The crazy guy was Mariama's lookalike brother. Their look works better on Mariama though, because Sullay's stocky build makes him look like a junior league boxer.

Mariama attempts to give Sullay the older sister glare that ends in a grin. He laughs and pats her on the head with the stack of papers in his hand. Like his sister, he makes up in personality what he lacks in height. He is charming and funny. Everyone loves Sullay. Especially his girlfriend Yinka who is now walking toward us with a smile that looks forced. Mariama lets out a loud groan. I turn to her and say "be nice!"

Mariama and Yinka tolerate each other. It is clear they both love Sullay. It is equally clear he doesn't quite know what to do with himself when he is with his two ladies. Yinka swings between warming up to Mariama and cooling off. Mariama thinks Yinka takes herself too seriously and so enjoys egging her on. She once told me that Yinka thinks only her opinions should matter when it comes to Sullay, as if she knows better. That, Mariama said, was the perfect trigger for her northern sensitivities. All Yinka needed to do was to say "wetin you tink" - *what do you think* - after making her declarations and it would be fine between them. "She needs to know I am Sullay's older sister and always will be!"

To which I had replied: "Yes oh Thara!" *Thara* - the term for Big Sister in Mariama's Temne, the name and language for the second largest ethnic group in the country.

Yinka squeezes in beside Sullay to receive his bear hug and kiss on the forehead before saying "Hey Sia, Mariama, ow una dae do?" *How are you doing?* if it was possible for Krio to sound proper, Yinka pulled it off. "Wetin una dae do na ya?!" - *what are you doing here* - she continued.

Mariama smiles sweetly and responds: "Kushe Yinka! We bin dae go na Kortor shop for braid" *Heya Yinka - We were going to the Fullah-guy's shop for bread*

"But Sullay, jus say una go go buy and bring am for we. So we go see una na room." *But Sullay just said you two lovebirds will go buy it and bring it to our room for us.*

She continues sweetly: "Una try ya...we don angry en get for eat befo de party!" *Please hurry! We are hungry and have to eat before the party!*

Yinka let out a weak "oh!" Sullay scowled at Mariama looking boyish and sheepish.

Mariama squeezes his arm and says: "tenke broda" - *thanks brother* - before doing an about face turn, pulling me along with her.

We both start laughing as soon as we round the corner away from them as we head back up the hill towards the Stone and our dorms. We were in the Lati Hyde Foster building. Lati Hyde Foster, was the first woman to attend this Fourah Bay College, then known as the Athens of West Africa, in the 1940s. She'd go on to be the Principal of the Annie Walsh Memorial Secondary School, reputed to be the oldest secondary school for girls in Sub-Saharan Africa. The other female dorm was called Beethoven - I've never understood that. It's one of the reasons Mariama and I opted to stay in Lati Hyde instead of moving into the senior dorm rooms we could have had in Beethoven as senior students.

~~~

We got up the long, steep flight of stairs that led to the Lati Hyde dorms. As we walked toward the entrance one of our flat-mates called out:

"Dem fine fine roomie dem!" *Hey beautiful roommates.*

Why did they keep trying to humor me?

In our room, we go to work to prepare for the night. We take out our small gas stove, set it on the balcony and heat our stew. We take out outfit choices and while Mariama putters around to refill our drinking water jug and clay pots, I get some homework done. Most faculties only have half-day classes if at all on Saturdays. As an Engineering student, I had classes all day. I really only had Sundays off and between classes and partying Friday and Saturday nights, I looked forward to Sundays with Aunty Kumba. Aunty Kumba, who was so proud of my being in Engineering, a feat that was not easy to accomplish in a system where many lecturers prided themselves on setting students up to fail. When I passed my first-year exams Aunty Kumba exclaimed: *You show you Papa say you pass any boy pikin!" You showed your dad you are worth much more than any son!* Sahr had started in Engineering but failed his first-year exams. Instead of taking his second-chance reference exams that summer, he had switched to Arts. After I passed, I told Aunty Kumba how one of my lecturers
~~~

had told me I needed to sleep with him if I wanted to pass the exams. I made him a deal that if I passed I would meet him at the rendezvous spot he kept for those occasions. Luckily for me, he got a scholarship for a research fellowship in the UK just after our exams. I later heard he was accused of sexual harassment by a student and almost lost his funding.

This week at Aunty Kumba's will be no different. I will arrive zonked out and hit her couch or bed. She had given up trying to make me go to church with her. She'll call out "ar go pray for you!" *I will pray for you* as she leaves. Four hours later when she arrives from the unnecessarily protracted service, I'll just be rousing enough for a shower and my first meal of the day. I'll listen to her ramble on about who was at church, complain about the 10 offerings that were made and then share the amazing testimonies she'd heard that day. I notice that lately I was getting more curious about these stories. They seem too good to be true so I am swinging between outright disbelief, skepticism and a nagging thought - what if these stories are true?

I'll doze off again with Aunty Kumba's voice lulling me to sleep. By evening, I will be awake again and it'll be my turn to share campus gossip while I pack the food bowls she'll have prepared for me and empty her groceries and a dress or two into a Ghana Must Go canvas bag before heading back to campus. We often fit in a stop to see my sister, Little Kumba at her boarding school too. And sometimes when Aunty Kumba and I have enough time and cash sent by my dad, we'd go by the corner bar that had just opened near her house, or head to Lumley Beach. I much preferred going to the bar which was called - *No Condition is Permanent - NCiP*. It was on the corner of St Johns and Campbell Street, which was a city center hub. When I was there, I knew it didn't matter much to the neighborhood customers that I was an FBC Engineering student. It felt like life was simpler there. In my almost-world though, making an appearance at Lumley Beach on Sunday evening was the thing to do. So we went there when we could.

I smile thinking of Aunty Kumba while I pack my books away ready for class in the morning. We'll be partying till daybreak so I'll only have time to get to our room to shower, change and head to class. Mariama and I get to trying outfits. We settle on fitted jeans and a black blouse for me. The off-shoulder blouse was an Aunty Kumba hand-me-down that was made for slightly smaller breasts, so some adjustments are needed. Mariama fiddles with my top, trying to adjust my size D boobs so that the fabric will stay comfortably high enough to show a bit of cleavage but not fall too low. We are going for sexy, not tacky, so we pin the stretchy fabric under the arms even tighter together. We just manage to get the top to where we are happy with it when there is a loud, quick, knock on the door.

Mariama calls out: "Sullay bo na you?! Cam insaiye bo we don angry so!" *Sullay is that you - come on in we are so hungry!*

The door opens and instead of Sullay, in walks Mohamed, who can only be described as tall, dark and handsome. I still have a hard time trying not to gawk at him even though he is 200 percent Mariama's. They only have eyes for each other. My pet name for them is M-Square.

Med, as we call him, let out a whistle, followed by: "Titi you fine oh!" *Girl you fine!* "Looking good Sia!"

I stoop down to pick up my shoes to hide my flushed reaction to his charming self. I murmur "bo lef bo! Wait tey you see you yone gyal tiday" *Stop it! Wait till you see your girl tonight.*

By the time, I straighten up, there they are, entangled in a deep kiss. I hear Med say "How's my Queen?" There's a muffled response from Mariama.

"Bo una sef una wait make ar go na do bo!" *Can you two wait until I leave please!* I quickly change in the dark of the balcony, grab my slippers and leave the room. Exiled - as we call it, to give them room for their lust-making.

A pang of longing hits me as I head down the corridor toward our other friend and flat mate Janice's room. In my almost-world, I had also almost had a real boyfriend. We were doing fine until I realized that the fool assigned numbers to his "serious underground programs." I was UG #3 because "eh smart but dem see am dae eat cookery na NCiP" *She's smart but she's been seen eating cooked street food at NCiP*. It had been easy to walk away from that guy.

~~~

When I walk into Janice's room, she also has her boyfriend, Harold Massaquoi there. I am struck by the contrast between the steamers I'd left behind and the coolness between this pair. Their relationship is like Harmattan. Predictable and cool. And just like the harmattan winds from the Sahara leaves a hazy dust cloud in the air, things are shady with these two. I was pretty sure that Janice is with Harold to prove to her conservative Creole family that she can do anything she wants. Janice is in the Arts and a leader in making feminist thinking conscious within the student body. She is also Janice Cole, of the Cole family, that has a pew at Trinity Church and who is expected to marry into another pewed family. The son of the Johnsons or Hamiltons, who was in the same Holy Communion Confirmation class as her. She once told me that after she told her family she was dating Harold, her grandmother had exclaimed: *"Lord oh! Tell God tenki at least whey not to some Muslim country-boy!" Thank God at least that he isn't a Muslim Provincial boy!* Harold is from the Provinces, but grew up in Freetown and is a Christian.

I'm also pretty sure that Harold is likewise with Janice because she'll serve his future political ambitions and get him Freetown votes and credibility. Harold is a political science and philosophy major. He is also a Mende, from the largest ethnic group in the country and a Bo School boy. Bo school is the renowned secondary school for boys named after the southern town of the
~~~

same name. Bo School produces highly intellectual students, often with political aspirations, who stereotypically use the biggest English words and phrases to say the simplest things. That's how Harold had won the current Student Union Presidency. People loved big English on this campus even when it means nothing.

Harold said: "Hey Sia, welcome! Janice, please express your thinking to Sia, about your hypothetical theoretical response to how you will navigate, if, by serendipitous happenstance, I decided to return to my chiefdom, to accept a chieftaincy after we have said our nuptials!"

Yesterday, Janice and Harold were debating what might happen if he decided to "abandon colonial, imperial, hegemonic thought and exercise his traditional rights to be polygamous." The day before, it was what his platform would be "to end nepotism, tribalism and all the isms in Africa in the eventuality he torpedoed quickly to higher office."

I will M-square to be quick.

~~~

Half an hour later I'd had enough of Harold and Janice. I bade them farewell till the party and head back to check whether M-square were done their business. I run into Yinka who awkwardly hands me the bread that Sullay asked her to deliver and sulks off. I'm relieved to see the lights on under our room door and hear Mariama say "de do open" *the door's open*, in response to my triple knock signal.

When I walk in, Mariama is changed for the party. She has chosen the red knee-length dress. No boob-adjustments needed for her size B cups and the form-fitting dress falls perfectly over her rounded butt. She whispers a coy: "tenke roomie!" *thanks roomie* - wearing a blush that only another dark-skinned woman can see behind her shiny, yet glazed-over eyes. I stick my tongue out at her
~~~

and give her the finger, which transforms into a grin and wave when Med emerges from the balcony to acknowledge my return. I help Mariama style her braids into an up-do and then shoo them to the balcony so I can change. Fifteen minutes later, I am back in my jeans and blouse. I slip on red pumps that are comfortable enough to dance in and wear matching red lipstick - the only makeup that was practical for partying in the African humidity and all the body heat that will be rising from the dancehall. My hair is permed straight and I slick it back into a boob framing my cheeks. I slip a hairband onto my wrist as well. I'd need it later when I want to pull my sweaty hair off my face and into a short puffy bun. M-square and I eat and chat a bit longer. At midnight, we leave and head to the pre-party gathering of We-Yone Club and friends outside the Student Union (SU) building where the party would happen. The night had just begun.

~~~

Three hours later, the party is in full swing. There we are: M-square, Yinka and Sullay, Janice and Harold and I, with so many other friends around us, dancing the night away. We, are invincible, and on top of the world. We couldn't be happier.

♪ ♪ *Boogie and Boogie and Boogie and Whine. Lord have Mercy!* ♪ ♪

I watch my friends singalong and dance the whine together. A moment of sadness washes over me as I dance alone or with whichever guy whines by. That's when I look up and see the student from Kalamazoo, Michigan, dancing offbeat, on his own, across from me. I'm surprised by the flash of recognition that courses through me as I watch the disco lights play with his pale hair and skin. We were both in almost-worlds - belonging and yet not. That's when I think to hell with it and cross the room to claim him for the night. He let me pull him close and lead him as I teach him how to move with the beat, and do the whine. Little did I know that because of this man, I would find refuge in America.
~~~

Our first signal of what was to come would arrive in exactly 3 hours from now, around 6am, when Aunty Kumba will arrive to interrupt our revelry. She will explain to me through tears as we stand outside the SU building with the dawn breaking, that rebels of the Revolutionary United Front had attacked Kono. They had targeted my parents' bed and breakfast. Tamba resisted and was shot and killed. My parents barely escaped with their lives and sustained wounds. They lost Finda in the shuffle. Thankfully, Aunty Kumba just heard through another friend that Finda was captured but escaped before the rebels could take her all the way to their bush base. I would vomit all over Aunty Kumba before fainting, the news curdling with the alcohol coursing through me and altogether too much to stomach.

Exactly two years from now, we will be flung further into a world that we are unprepared for. We will leave another party to find out that the rebels have entered Freetown and announced that they are heading to our campus to "deal with those students." I will look on in shock, fear, betrayal and hopelessness as United States Special Forces will arrive on campus out of no-where, to evacuate my Kalamazoo. I'd be screaming when a soldier will pick me up, throw me into a truck and speed away. It won't be until we arrive at the helipad that I will realize I was taken by the US special forces and not rebels. My Kalamazoo told them I was his wife. We'd just married that week and hadn't picked up the marriage certificate. And I was pregnant, which meant I was carrying an American citizen. He told me we were being taken to Guinea, Conakry for temporary visas to be issued for people like me, but that I am to say I "miscarried from the shock" if they want to do a pregnancy test. Once in the US, we will quickly marry for real. After all that sinks in, I'll start screaming all over again, thinking of my parents, little Kumba, Finda, Aunty Kumba and my friends left behind.

My parents, Little Kumba and Finda will make it out to Guinea by road. Little Kumba was with them because they were in

Freetown on business and because it was a Sunday, she'll plan to stay the night with them before heading back to boarding school the next day. Her boarding school will be raided and many students raped and abducted. Aunty Kumba still shares Little Kumba serendipitous escape as a testimony of God's intervention. Aunty Kumba will survive by living common-law with a big politician who'll send his family abroad to safety, while staying to side with the rebels in hopes of securing a seat in the coalition government. He'll eventually leave her when his wife will return minus their kids and Aunty Kumba will move on to be kept by a Nigerian Captain from the West African intervention force that will help end the war.

M-square will make it separately to The Gambia, where they'll reunite and marry. Janice and Harold end up in Australia. Harold will get there first and marry and sponsor Janice to join him. Harold will become a Pastor and Janice a Women's Studies Professor. Sullay will never leave but will live to tell stories no young man should have to tell. Yinka will go to the UK with her parents. Sullay will be distraught when he finds out that she marries his good friend Jalloh. Jalloh, who'll get mysteriously wealthy and will become a "businessman" travelling back and forth between London and several central African countries. And in the happily ever after, my Kalamazoo and I will have three beautiful brown-skinned children, with heads full of big dark curls. We will raise them in the same City of Kalamazoo, Michigan, where Dad grew up, and where black describes me and them but not Dad.

But for tonight, black only means the color of the blouse I am wearing. And right now, we are young, innocent and free. We are swinging, swaying, in unison with our pseudo-adulthood and with each other. We are invincible and on top of the world, with not one care as we belt along with Nancy Martinez:

♪ ♪ *What else can I do*
Cause For Tonight

(Oooh, aaah)
A little love and candlelight
(Oooh, aaah)
For Tonight
(Oooh, aaah)
A little love and candlelight
Can't we be in love for just one night!!! ♪ ♪

4 THE RAINBOW

"Mummy?"

"Mummy?"

"Huh?" I responded absentmindedly. My thoughts raced to what remained of the day, cataloging and running through the checklist for the evening. *Make dinner, pack lunches, check homework, fold laundry, check email.* The tasks of the evening were all vying for space at the forefront of my mind as we trudged through the fallen grass, walking across the soccer field to the car.

"Why do bad things happen? Why do children suffer and die?"

My mind squeaked to a halt. My mother's heart suddenly started the jolting fall of an aging elevator, seemingly dropping in seconds all the way to my feet and then taking a slow, steady ascent back to its compartment in my ribcage, where it started thumping so loudly, I was sure she could hear it. The instant moisture on my forehead and palms matched the droplets of moisture so beautifully spread out and nestled on the fallen leaves all around us.

It was a beautiful, autumn day. It was one of those days that fills you with the wonder and awe of the creation we are part of, complete with the recipe of autumn sunshine and rains mixed together. In an hour, dark clouds would appear, and then be washed away and replaced with the brightest blue ones. The leaves and trees were filled with vibrant hues of red, yellow, purple, orange and brown, replacing the chlorophyll-filled greenery of summer leaves. The season was changing around us, as it was for my beautiful innocent child. Was this the moment I had prepared for these 6 years since 2014? It was 2020 and she was now 8 years old, right at that age of curiosity and wonder when questions were no longer rhetorical, childish statements. Questions were questions, and they required thoughtful answers.

As if reading my thoughts, she piped up again - this time tugging at my shirt, her expectant eyes peering into my shifting ones, searching for a response: "Huh Mummy? It's so terrible. Why?"

We were walking slower now. She, in anticipation of a response and I, unable to move at my normal brisk pace, because my feet had colluded with my thumping heart and the growing knot in my stomach to slow me down. I turned to face my daughter, as she simultaneously pivoted ninety degrees to face me. The sunlight bathed her face and I gasped at her beauty. Her eyes were almond shaped, dark and striking. Her eye brows, black and full, were perfectly arched, exactly the shape I get mine threaded into at the Indian salon in the strip mall we frequented. Her skin was as smooth as a baby's, a dark hue of milk chocolate.

Her cornrows framed her oval face perfectly. The five strips I'd braided sideways in the front fell over her left temple, while the rows in the back crisscrossed until they came together into the shape of an open flower at the top of her head. The braided lengths actually looked like petals – because her thick curly hair was held too loosely to be tamed with the hair elastic that was meant to hold them together for the soccer game she was supposed to be playing. Instead, the lengths fell open, falling this way and that, forming their own shapes, as stubborn and beautiful as the head they crowned.

She was smiling as she watched me take stock of her. Her lips were full and her upper lip curled upward when she smiled, her double dimples further drawing attention to her high cheek bones. She was gorgeous, this child.

My Ebola child.

She reached for my face, her fingertips gently stroking my cheek, and then predictably, her fingers started exploring. I felt the tears well up at the back of my eyes. The clouds were dark again, as if to match my mood, and a tentative drizzle drop fell on my cheek, as if to encourage my tears to fall.

I guess today was the day I would have to tell her that she was representative of the question she'd asked. Today, I would have to tell her that the very gesture of her fingers on my face was how she had adopted us. She'd been so traumatized by sitting in an Ebola isolation ward in Sierra Leone with no human contact, that when she was pronounced Ebola free, she'd rejected all connection. She had refused to look at or touch anyone. Then we'd walked into the orphanage that was her temporary home. We were unsure why we were there, but were drawn from an inner cry to help the children who'd become pariahs in the dust of the Ebola plague that had swept the region.

Some of the children were truly orphaned, their parents and entire households swept away with the Ebola epidemic. Some however, had immediate and extended family who 6 months after the official end of the outbreak refused to reclaim them. Government officials along with Doctors Without Borders and Red Cross volunteers would show up as part of the family tracing program to ask relatives to take a child of their family lineage into their homes. More often than not, they were told: 'I don't know this child.' Some did this because they were too poor to feed another mouth; others, because they believed that the children of Ebola victims would bring bad luck and may get reinfected. Sadly, communities who didn't want the '*Ebola children,'* as they were called, corroborated the denials.

Our daughter fit both categories, orphaned and unclaimed. Yet as we stood there, the social worker talking to us about our volunteer role and the routine for bathing and feeding the children, suddenly started jumping up and down. She clapped her hands and uttered the Krio phrase 'Lord, oh!!!' to express her amazement. Our daughter, who'd spoken to and touched no one, and consistently turned away from those who approached her, walked across the room, straight to Dad. She raised her arms to be picked up, peering into his face, then over at mine. Then she reached across, and touched my face, resting her tiny, gentle, trembling fingers on my cheek for a few moments, before letting them roam to explore the rest of my face. Our tears flowed freely as we were told the story of this 2-year old Ebola survivor - a miracle in every way. We took her to our family home in Sierra Leone that day. A year later, we came back, adoption papers in hand and brought her to our home in Beautiful British Columbia, Canada.

I smiled as she continued to trigger memories with her fingers, much surer now than they'd been 6 years ago. I'd have to tell her that her recurring dreams of 'the astronauts in yellow suits' were actually memories of the health workers in protective gear. They'd tried to save her parents and cared for her in that rancid isolation ward, crawling with Ebola-infested feces, vomit and blood. I'd tell her how she had started crying unexpectedly at her first swimming lesson, until we realized the smell of chlorine must remind her of her chlorinated freedom bath – the bath Ebola survivors got to be decontaminated before they left quarantine. We'd stopped the swimming lesson that day, and I'd stood by with bated breath when she'd asked to rejoin her lessons weeks afterwards. I was thankful the second lesson was uneventful. I'd have to explain to my gorgeously beautiful and smart daughter that it was because of her ordeal, we could now simply get Ebola vaccines on our trips to Sierra Leone every other summer – because too many other men, women and children just like her had died before the world took notice and fast-tracked the drug and vaccine development for Ebola, a virus that had existed 38 years before the outbreak that she survived.

I had no excuse. Her soccer game was cancelled because the fields were too wet from the on and off rains of the past 3 days. We were alone. Dad and the other 3 children were not expecting us for an hour.

"Well…" I heard myself say through lips that suddenly felt dry, stiff and heavy.

Whatever words were about to come from my lips were interrupted by a squeal of sheer delight.

"Look, look, mummy!"

The sun had broken through the clouds again, and there, so close, clear and textured that I was sure we could reach out and touch it, was the brightest, most beautiful rainbow I had ever seen. Suddenly, we were both laughing as we simultaneously dived into my handbag in search of the new iPhone xtra, to take a 3D picture that'll have us look like we were in the rainbow. Snap, snap. And off we raced to the car.

As we strapped in, she said, "Mum, you didn't answer my question, though."

I smiled a calm, assured smile. My words flowed freely, effortlessly now, "Well, baby, remember the story of Noah and the rainbow?..."

5 BACK TO THE BEGGINING

Mariama sat and stared at the flickering flame of the fireplace. She was captivated by the way the flames danced and moved. It was so hard to believe that these dancing flames were not real. This electric fireplace, a veneer, just like what her life had slowly become in this place. Here in Canada, where she'd found refuge, but she feared she was losing her mind and losing herself. The flickering flames suddenly bothered her and she closed her eyes. Even then, she found no solace in the dark as her mind replayed in vivid color this day, that day, and all the other days that were all jumbled together sometimes.

She opened her eyes again and tried to remember why she had come downstairs to the living room at 1:00am, while Med and the kids were sound asleep. She looked at the bottle of Tylenol 3's in her hand, a little shocked that she was holding it because she couldn't feel any pain anywhere. At least no physical pain. The jumbled images were still floating around her even with her eyes open. She willed herself to get up and go upstairs but couldn't make her body move. She gave up and curled into a fetal position on the couch. She was finding out why people in pain defaulted to fetal positions. It was comfortable, this fetal place. Perhaps it was also the signal that rebirth might be possible if you stay there long enough.

~~~
~~~

It was the year 2000. Mariama stretched as she heard the call to morning prayer. It was the sound she'd woken up to every morning in Port Loko, Northern Sierra Leone as a child, so for her it was a comforting sound. Her father was the Chief, and they lived right next to the mosque. Islam was her family's faith but her dad never required that she join with the women for morning prayer as a child. She started joining her mom and step-moms in her early teens just to please him. Theirs was a special, silent bond. She knew simply by a look from him, a wink, a smile, a somber nod, how far she could push against the walls of tradition. He called her his Bathe - favored one. He treated her with the rights of a first born, even though it would have been normal for him to give her birthright to her brother, who even though he was second born, would have first-born son privileges.

Her uncles and others would often tell him to stop indulging her but he'd refuse to discuss his parenting decisions with them. For that, she loved him. In a place where everyone knew and was in each other's business, it felt good to be above scrutiny. She pitied her dad his plight though - being a Chief in rapidly changing modern times. What a conundrum! So she chose her battles carefully. She tried to keep some weight off him by doing things to please him, to compensate for the controversies she inevitably provoked. She had too much of a mind and voice of her own.

Her dad had sent her to school with his son, Sullay, because he felt education was important for all children in this age. So off they went, herself and Sullay to the Catholic Mission School across town because it was the best in town while all their younger siblings went to the school closer to home. They were the oldest, he explained, and would both inherit chieftaincy responsibilities from him. At the end of Form 5 though, her uncles started dropping hints. What would Sullay study that he can bring back to support the town's business. Perhaps law at Fourah Bay College? Maybe medicine? Surely, he would go all the way to a doctorate. They didn't even care what the doctorate would be in - just that their son and chief's heir came back learned from his studies. There was no mention of her studying further.

Then came the proposal - they thought she should marry Alimamy Bai Bureh, the sub-chief. What a great political move that would be? It would solidify the whole chiefdom and she would be an asset in negotiations given her education. Mariama recalled her horror when she heard the news. She told Papa that she would run away if he didn't get her out of it. What about Halima, surely, she would make a better bride? He'd simply said sternly – "Leave it with me." A week later there was an announcement – Halima was betrothed to sub-Chief Alimamy. She, Mariama, will be Freetown-bound with Sullay to attend Fourah Bay College (FBC), the University of Sierra Leone. Mariama had been elated, but felt guilty for suggesting Halima. She hadn't meant it - Halima was just the first name that had come to her in the heat of the moment.

Halima was her first cousin and a year behind her in school. Marriage meant she wouldn't even finish secondary school. Mariama avoided Halima the week of the announcement. When she could avoid her no more, she went to see her the morning of the traditional wedding. Mariama was greeted by a stunning, glowing woman, instead of a young, cowering, sad or angry bride. Her cousin Halima had blossomed overnight, clearly enjoying the attention as all the women waited on her. She presided over it all perfectly. She'd looked at Halima and said with serene grace in Temne, their ethnic language: "Mariama, conne karange. Me nor, eh ye do yen" *Mariama, go learn. Me, I belong here.* Halima would go on to make an exceptional chief's wife and improve conditions for women in her chiefdom for years to come.

The call to prayer was done. That meant Mariama had another 30 minutes before she needed to get ready for work. She hugged her pillow. She cherished these simple things. Sleeping, waking without the sounds of gunshots, hugging a pillow, breathing in air that didn't smell of fear, or sweat or dried blood, or human feces, or corpses – the smells of war. She thought of Mohammed now, her Med. It had been so hard to leave him behind in Freetown.

She had met Med, the week that she and Sullay arrived in Freetown to attend FBC in 1994. They were finishing their registration on campus the week of orientation when Med walked by, tall, dark and handsome. She noticed him immediately. There was a casual arrogance about him that drew her like a magnet. He had stopped to talk to some other students. He suddenly lifted his head to catch her stare. Mariama had tried to look away, but his gaze was intoxicating. He openly stared back, taking her in and letting his eyes wander over her before smiling lazily, as if he already knew she was his. She expected him to approach her but he didn't. He broke their gaze and turned back to his chatting. Mariama was confused – she'd always been called beautiful and was used to being approached by men.

The next time they ran into each other they again shared a gaze and he was the one to break it and walk away. The third time, Mariama was just about to walk over to him, her striking oval eyes flashing mad, when he made the move towards her in what seemed like 3 strides of his long legs. He'd greeted her with a simple: "Hello Queen." She tried to play it hard to get, but only lasted two weeks. The rest, as they say, is history. They soon became couple number one on campus.

By the time rebels of the Revolutionary Union Front (RUF) entered Freetown and arrived at campus in 1999 to terrorize students, she and Med were inseparable. Just an hour before the rebels stormed the campus, her best friend and roommate Sia was evacuated with her boyfriend Nick, an American exchange student from Kalamazoo, Michigan. Mariama remembers Nick whispering a strangled "I'm so sorry" as the American Special Forces took him and Sia. When Mariama closed her eyes and listened, she could still hear the sounds of her and Sia's screams as they were separated. Sia had looked mildly insane in that moment – like she didn't understand what was happening. Moments later, she was gone with the harmattan winds blowing on that January morning, leaving only the skid marks of the military trucks that took them. Mariama remembers Med's voice bringing her back from staring at the truck tracks. They had to make a run for it. The rebels would be there any moment. There was a bush road around the back of the botanical gardens behind the science building. They'd go that way and through back roads until they made it to the West-end of town where it was safe from ground fighting.

They didn't make it out of campus before the rebels arrived just after noon, so they'd lain in the bushes of the botanical gardens, watching for snakes while they heard rebels yelling, laughing and shooting. They heard female students screaming and a male student who tried to argue shot. They heard windows and other things smashed as the whole campus was vandalized. They lay there while the students that were rounded up were made to chant for 3 hours nonstop "We love RUF!" At some point, Med had shifted and covered her with his body, shielding her ears with his hands. She sobbed silently into the dirt as stray bullets flew past them. She used to complain that she didn't understand expressions like the 'smell of fear.' It was then that she realized she could indeed smell fear. The air was thick with it. She'd realized later that she wet herself as they lay there.

Six hours later, the rebels had also sped off in their trucks, taking students with them. They also took away the innocence and scarred a generation forever. Mariama and Med had lain there for another hour until they heard others come out of hiding and were sure some rebels hadn't been left behind to capture those who emerged. Med didn't want them to risk it. They would find their way down the mountain and through the back roads now even though it was getting dark and dangerous. He had a hunch the rebels would come back. They would later find out Med's hunch was right. Rebels had returned and raped, killed or maimed the students who they found still hiding out on campus.

When they arrived in the West-end a day and a half later they were filthy, tired and starving. They'd only had water along the way. They didn't have many connections in the West-end – most of their relatives were in the East-end. Like Mariama, Med's family was from the North. They found shelter in a tin shack together for 2 weeks before they ran into a college buddy who'd escaped campus as well. His family lived on Collegiate Road in the West. He took them in. Although there was no ground fighting and daily terrorism in the West-end, there was no food. East-end was the commercial district where all the markets were. The bombing was also severe in the West. They got adept at gauging the sounds that preceded the bombs so they knew when to take shelter. Once, the house next to them was shelled and they spent an afternoon digging through debris to rescue the 2 young men who were trapped in it. By the time they got to them, the one who was trapped on top of the other had passed away.

Eventually, they found a new routine. Mariama went to the closest first aid centre to volunteer every day and Med would go about town with a group of friends to scavenge for food. Mariama got lots of extra food and supplies from working with the aid workers. Med and company often brought home delicacies - they'd taken to breaking into the West-end supermarkets that had been hastily locked-up before their owners left town. It was the only way to survive. Once they had ventured too far across town into rebel lines and one of the guys was shot. He survived with flesh wounds but then on the way back, the West African intervention force thought he was a rebel and shot him before Med and the others could confirm his identity. They were shaken and that's when Mariama and Med decided they needed to find a way out.

A week afterwards, the aid workers told Mariama they were leaving for Gambia and could take her. They could verify her identity to Gambian immigration authorities and had recommended her as a good volunteer to their organization. There was an offer of a job with basic room and board for her in Gambia. She would be working at the distribution office there. They could only take her though, so at first, she refused. She could not leave Med behind. But Med convinced her to go. She had to leave. He was a guy he said. The worse that could happen to him was that his hand might be cut off - a favorite atrocity of the rebels. He could not bear the thought of what might happen to her. Eventually, the whole household convinced her to leave.

She rubbed her hand over her bulging stomach, the fruit of their lovemaking the night before Mariama left. Mariama held back tears now as she tried not to despair. She had not heard from Med in 3 weeks, which was extremely unusual. It was difficult calling home, but they had gotten accustomed to talking at least once a week. Mariama would call the phone centre guy in Freetown and if she went through, would ask him to tell Med to be there at a certain time later in the week when she'll call back. Med's routine was to stop by for messages daily so he always knew when to come back to talk to her. They were excited about the baby, but didn't dare hope too much about being together soon or before the baby was born.

Things were getting better in Freetown and the country overall. The government and intervention force had gained ground from the rebels, but the war wasn't over yet. She had managed to find out that both her family in Port Loko and Med's family in Kabala had survived the Northern attacks. Her family went in and out of hiding but her dad refused to leave because he was the Chief. She also managed to talk to him periodically. He had said about her pregnancy after a pause on the phone, that his dream had not been for his Bathe to be without a degree, unmarried and pregnant, but that these were not usual times. She'd promised him she would finish school someday and make it - for all their sakes, she was determined to. Sullay had gone through many hard times in Freetown but was now volunteering with the United Nations Mission and at least making enough of a stipend to eat every day. Med's family had crossed the border and were in the refugee camp in Forecariah, Guinea. Med's mother's health wasn't good and she kept contracting all the infections that kept spreading across the camp.

Mariama wiped the tears rolling down her cheeks. She had to be strong for the baby. She would try calling the phone centre guy again today. An hour later, she was ready for work. She'd eaten breakfast and was walking to the office on Kankujereh Road. They had managed to get her basic lodging in a compound close enough to walk. She cherished the smell and sounds of peace as she walked. She'd made many friends with the market women and hawkers and enjoyed the greeting rituals every day on her morning walk. "Na'nga def," she'd call out to greet her new friends in Wolof. She had learnt enough phrases to get by.

Things were busy at the office that day and for that, Mariama was grateful. She didn't have time to think or fret about Med. Towards the end of the day though, she noticed a growing sense of urgency. She finished off her admin tasks in a hurry. She needed to get to the call centre before they closed. When she got there, the news was the same. No, the phone centre guy said when she got through to him, he hadn't heard from or seen Med at all. She could always try again tomorrow but he also was beginning to think something was wrong. Mariama forced back the tears that threatened to overflow as she stepped out of the phone booth at the centre. She couldn't let people see her pain. "Ba beneen mangi dem." She said the farewell greeting and quickly left before the centre attendant could ask her questions.

She cried all the way on the walk home for the first time in the 3 weeks of silence. She chose a different route so she wouldn't have to greet people on the way. She got to her compound and luckily it was evening prayer time and it was quiet because everyone was at prayers. She fumbled through her purse to find her keys, blinded by her tears. When she lifted her head, there, through the haze of her tears, she could make out a figure lurking by her door. She screamed. It must be a stalker or a thief and she was completely vulnerable with the compound empty. The figure stepped out of the shadows walking towards her. She saw the figure's mouth move and a second later heard "My Queen!" It was Med.

~~~

She heard the baby crying and Mariama squeezed her eyes shut. Surely it wasn't time for another feed yet. She felt like she'd just come to bed after the last feed and she was exhausted. She checked the time. It was 6am. That meant, she had indeed just come to bed an hour ago. She could see her ravenous baby through the monitor sucking his lips and thumbs vehemently as if he hadn't been fed for hours. He was so ready for another meal. Med was snoring loudly next to her. She begrudged him his snoring even though she knew he needed to be up in half an hour to get ready for work. Mariama's eyes closed again involuntarily and she started drifting off.

"Mariama! Bo go take da pikin nor!" *Mariama! Go pick up the baby!*

His tone jolted her awake and she felt an instant rage rising from the pit of her stomach.

"You okay?" She heard Med say, his voice muffled as if from a distance.

Mariama blinked to steady herself. She felt the rush of blood receding from her pounding head and the buzzing noise in her ears dim a little as she forced herself to focus. When she could focus enough to see Med's face, he was staring at her with a mixture of concern and irritation. She deciphered that she was sitting upright and staring at
~~~

him in an unfocused sleep-deprived rage.

Mariama broke her stare, suddenly feeling dejected. Without a word, she slipped out of bed and stood up wobbly. Baby was screaming louder now. She left their bedroom and walked over to the bedroom closest to theirs where baby slept. She resented this, her walk of shame, and cringed with every single step thinking of the fight she'd had with Med about moving baby to the next room.

He couldn't take it anymore he said - baby screaming in the room. He gets headaches when the baby cries at night and he wakes, making him useless at work in the morning.

She'll keep baby in the bed with her instead of the crib then, she said. That's much easier for her anyway she'd argued. She can just breastfeed through the night without getting up and then everyone sleeps better.

"Are you mad!" Med had retorted. What if he rolled over and choked baby at night?! And how was he to be with her while baby was in the bed?!

She had looked at him with cold disdain. She told him she would not argue with him anymore. Baby stays. She'd fumed all evening, unable to comprehend that all he cared about was how they could be together over her need to rest too.

That night, she went to bed with her back to Med's side, tucking baby close to her with pillows on the edge of the bed to prevent him from rolling. When she woke to breastfeed two hours later, she simply adjusted herself enough to hold her breast up for baby to latch onto the nipple. As soon as baby latched, she settled back to sleep comfortable. As she dozed off, she noted that Med had come to bed. She could feel the hardness of his back against hers. She had left him downstairs listening to Komla Dumor on BBC World News and had expected him to sleep on the couch with the

TV on. That's all he did these days - watch TV. Many years later when Komla Dumor would die unexpectedly young, she will feel a pang of guilt for having resented his voice.

She enjoyed a blissful week feeding baby through the night in the bed. She felt more rested in the morning, while Med looked angrier and angrier every day. A week later, she jolted awake from a bad dream. She dreamt that baby had rolled off the bed while she slept. She felt the damp of panic sweat on her forehead as she jolted awake, thankful it was a dream. Then she realized baby was not in the bed and was staring up at her wide-eyed and whimpering softly. She'd gotten lazy and stopped putting the pillow barrier on the edge of the bed. It was no dream. Baby had rolled and fallen off the bed. Luckily, baby had fallen on one of her pillows that had fallen on the floor earlier in the day. He was shocked but not hurt from the fall. She on the other hand was completely shaken. She was trembling with silent tears rolling down her cheeks as she examined him to make sure he was okay.

Later that day, she told Med about dropping baby and apologized for their fight. He simply glared at her and said "if anything happens to my son…." and walked away.

His son!

Sometimes she wondered if she even knew him anymore. She had moved baby that night to the other room. Now, the constant trekking back and forth through the nights left her depleted. The good news was she was much more awake when she sat in the feeding chair to breastfeed baby, she thought, as she rocked and fed baby now. She smiled as she scratched his tightly knit curls. What a joy it had been to receive this baby. Their Canadian baby. Their only son, Baby Mohamed aka Baby Mo.

Just then, she heard her Gambian babies awaken. There was Mariam her first born. Sweet Mariam their love-child conceived during the war. Her middle name was Blessing. And what a blessing she was! When Med arrived in Gambia after risking his life to be smuggled by road by truck drivers from Freetown all the way to Gambia, they were determined to make something of their lives. Med had gone through Guinea and stopped at the refugee camp in Forecariah to see his family. He'd instructed his dad that they should tell Mariama what he had set out to do if he never made it to Gambia. He hadn't told his mom what he was doing - she was ailing too fast. He was concerned for her and needed to send money to his dad for the medications they needed, he told Mariama. They'd sent all Mariama had saved but for what she needed for medical bills. Then Med hit the road looking for work.

He did anything - odd jobs, cleaning jobs at offices and kept networking, looking for business management jobs. He was a final year business student at FBC before the war broke, he'd explain to his bosses at his odd jobs. One day he plans to finish and get his MBA too. One of his bosses was an FBC alum from the generation of Gambians that had studied at FBC - The Athens of West Africa - when Gambia had no university of its own. He decided to help Mohammed. He saw the determination in him too and how hard he worked. He put him in charge of logistics in their supply chain business. Next, Med was doing the books. His books were so well done that when the KPMG accountants reviewed them, they asked about his background and offered him a bookkeeping job until he could finish his degree and chartered accountancy.

Eventually he finished his studies by taking night classes. They were elated. They had enough to send money home to both sides of their families and get a nanny for Mariam so Mariama could also return to work. The only dark cloud was that Med's mom didn't make it and had passed away about 3 months after Med arrived in Gambia. She died the week they got married and the week Mariam was born.

Soon they were pregnant again. Then came the most incredible offer they had never expected. KPMG North American needed some capacity - would Med consider a transfer abroad to Canada, his boss asked. They would sponsor the whole family including the new baby. Med would be on a work visa, but Mariama could get one too if she found work. After 2 years, if he liked it there, they could apply for permanent residency and choose to stay. There was no hesitation. They would go. It was two and a half years from that time before they would leave Banjul International Airport bound for Toronto's Pearson International Airport. By then, they'd had two more, not one more baby - the twins Isata and Isha. It was 2004 when they arrived in Toronto. Mariam was 3 and the twins were 1.

~~~

"Mummy! I can't find my school bag."

"Coming Mariam!"

"Give me my bottle!"

"That's not yours! It's mine!"

"Stop it twins!

"Mummy, Mummy, Baby Mo is crying!"

"Mariam, here's your bag - leave Baby Mo alone. He's fine!"

"He's not fine Mummy, he's crying"

"And you're not his mother Mariam! Twins! STOP it!"

"Daddyyyyyy"

"Mariam - talk to your mom - listen to her. I have to go!"

"Med!! At least strap the kids in the car before you leave! I'm putting baby in the car seat!"
~~~

buzzzzzz buzzzzz buzzzzz

"Mariam! Grab my cell phone!"

"Ok Mummy"

"Oh, hi Aunty Sia! Yes, we are going to the car now. We are late for school. No, Papa left a few minutes ago. Yes, that's Baby Mo screaming but mom says he's fine. Yes, I love kindergarten. Um hmm"

"Give me the phone Mariam!"

"Yes, Mummy - here."

"Hey Sia love. Sorry, I'll call you later...Girl, it's crazy. I don't know if I can do this anymore. It's crazy. No help! I'm the cook, the driver, the nanny, the cleaner. Now Med just left and didn't even strap the kids in the car and I have all these bags. Then he wants a wife at night…"

"Twins, STOP fighting!"

"What did you say? I know it'll get better, but it's not easy here oh! With four little kids, 5, 3 and 1 years old."

"STOP it girls!"

"Sia, how's Nick? Oh Papa? I spoke to Papa yesterday - he's just busy pressuring me to go back to school, but he and Mama need lots of money now. They're back in Port Loko and trying to rebuild. I have to get back to work soon…. STOP it girls...girls, get back down here we have to go! Sullay? Sullay is doing well but they need more support. Papa is taking on the land rights issue. He wants to leave the legacy of being the one to end the provincial land laws so Creoles will no longer be restricted from buying land in the provinces. I think it's audacious but I'm so worried about him. The other chiefs will crucify him!"

CRASH BANG CRASH ROLL CRASH

"WHAT the!..."

Isha was lying on the bottom of the stairs. A pool of blood was gathering behind her head. Isata was on the staircase landing covering her eyes and screaming. Mariama was running toward Isha. Baby Mo was sleeping peacefully in his car seat, sucking on his pacifier.

~~~

She only remembers flashing lights, white walls and the smell of ethyl alcohol. She didn't know how she got there. Mariam told her later she had called 911 because "Mummy you have always told me if anything happens call 911!" The social worker was talking to her. Isha will be fine. It is just a concussion and a really nasty gash at the back of her head. They are wondering though - would she like to have some help with Mariam and the twins. If she voluntarily signed they could take them away for a while to give her relief and help. They knew about the postpartum depression. It is on her file that her doctor had referred her to a counselor and psychologist but she had refused the follow-ups to schedule the consultations. She screamed at the social worker. "How dare you ask to take my kids away! How dare you!"

Med rushed in saying Aunty Sia had called him and told him what happened. She tensed up and looked at him imploringly, her large eyes screaming: *will you forgive me?* The way he'd been behaving lately, she expected him to slap her or something. That would actually be welcome she'd thought. She could use some punishment right now. She needed to feel some pain. Med took what seemed like 3 long strides towards her. He looked stern and handsome at the same time. AT first, she couldn't read him. Then she realized that he looked pained. He mouthed: "my Queen!" And pulled her into an embrace where she broke down like a popsicle collapsing at noon in 35-degree Sierra Leonean heat.
~~~

~~~

She wasn't sure if she'd been dozing and dreaming or awake and letting the memories fade in and out. It didn't matter. The light was filtering through the windows now and she could hear the soft sounds of the morning coming. Even the birds are more civilized here, she thought. Chirping quietly and getting louder very gradually as if to wake their human companions gently. She stretched out on the couch and slowly stood up. The birds had succeeded in rousing her. She walked to the kitchen and put the Tylenol 3's away before heading to the bathroom to pee. She sat on the toilet for what seemed like a very long pee. It smelled. And so did she – a mixture of morning breath and the balmy sweat of her reveries. She wiped herself and examined the stains on the toilet paper before flushing it and standing up. She stared at her reflection. She didn't like what she saw. Her roots were grown so much that her braids hung limply without form. Her oval eyes were sunken, her face puffy.

She climbed the steps slowly and stopped by the girls' room. They were all sound asleep. Isha looked peaceful and pain-free. Mariama was so thankful. She loved watching them sleep, loved hearing their soft snoring. If only for their sake, she thought, I have to make it. In their bedroom, Med was snoring loudly. She closed her eyes and welcomed the sound, remembering the times in Gambia she longed to wake up to his snoring. It was the first time in years his snoring did not annoy her. She stood and looked at him for a very long time. *We need to make it. We have come too far.* Memories of their steamy college nights flooded her, also for the first time in, well, years. She felt herself get damp between her legs. They'd been like African heat together. How had they let the snow and winter of this place creep into their marriage?

She went into their bathroom and brushed her teeth. She had stopped caring about herself or her body. But she would take care of herself today she decided. Thank God it was Saturday. She'd start by
~~~

undoing her braids and redoing them. She wouldn't leave them in so long anymore. In the shower, she took her mom's advice and prayed. What did she have to lose? Her mother, was now secretly a Christian and spending a lot of time with the missionaries in Port Loko. She'd convinced the missionary women to stop thinking of the Muslim townswomen as pagans and to come to evening prayers so that they can sit and talk and learn from each other afterwards. So she showered and prayed for a while.

She finally stepped out of the shower, wiped down and put on some deodorant, then her favorite perfume. She went to bed naked and inched under the covers, lying on her back. She turned to look at Med as he stirred. He lifted his head partially, looking at her with concern in his eyes. "You okay?" he asked. "Better" she answered. She saw his eyes flash as he realized she was naked in bed. She had stopped doing that a long time ago. He slowly placed a limp hand on her stomach, asking permission with his eyes. Her eyes welled up for a second, his tentativeness saddening her. She used to love how he'd claim her without hesitation. She had taken away his open rights to her. When she looked at him and smiled he started making circles on her navel, slowly inching larger rings downwards to where her heat was rising. They both groaned simultaneously as a very loud "Mummy!" rang out from the girls' room.

Mariama looked at Med and said: "Here's the plan. I need you to get the kids, brush their teeth – and yours - and take them downstairs. Put the Sesame Street box set on and give them their bowls of cereal in front of the TV. They love Sesame Street and don't move while it's on. I need you to make sure baby is strapped down in the high-chair – we don't need any more accidents. Then put the baby monitor on."

She drew in a breath and reached for his part that was alert like a mic, waiting to be held and sung to. Rubbing gently, she said: "After that, I want you to come back up here, lock the door, and take me back to the beginning. Come fuck me like you used to."

Med's eyes shone in recognition, shock and a flood of relief. He bolted out of the bed and hit the door just as one child reached it. She heard him hustling them and grinned, wondering if she'd still be awake by the time he got back.

6 THE DAY AUNTY AMIE DIED

It didn't feel right that the phone was ringing. I reached blindly for my cell phone, knocking over the glass of water I'd left on the nightstand before bed. *Crap!* I straightened up on my elbows, a bit more awake now. 3:05 am. That meant it was most likely a call from home and if so, there were only two possibilities. Some inconsiderate relative had gotten a hold of my number and was calling to ask me to send money or something else for them. Or, something was wrong. I answered the phone and heard my father's voice from across the oceans in Freetown, Sierra Leone:

"Hi Samuel. I know I'm waking you up."

"Oh, Morning Papa." I was holding my breath. "Is everything ok? Is Mama fine?"

"Yes, Mama is fine. It's your Aunty Amie who passed away this morning here. We are arranging for the funeral. I need you to send a couple of hundred dollars for funeral expenses."

"Ok. I will send $500?" I offered.

"Yes, that should do."

"Ok Papa. I will send it today and text you details"

"Borbor (*Young man*), just call. I've told you I don't see the text messages on this phone."

"Ok." I countered, trying not to sound irritated at his refusal to use any messaging. There was a pause. "Papa?"

"Yes, son?"

"Sorry about Aunty Amie." I said.

"It's ok son. It's her time and God's will. Go back to sleep. I know you have work in the morning." There was a click as he hung up and the phone went dead.

I stared at the phone for a couple of seconds, noticing I felt strangely dispassionate about the news. There was only a blank nothingness. I mopped up the water on the nightstand with a tee-shirt that was on the floor by my bedside. I checked to make sure my alarm was still set for 5:30am before I set the phone back on the nightstand and fell right back to sleep.

~~~

When my alarm went off, I was already awake and expecting it. Like clockwork, my body seemed to wake up 5 minutes before the alarm went off every day. I jumped out of bed, changed and headed downstairs to the gym in my building. I greeted the usuals who were already there doing their morning workouts and went ahead with mine. Treadmill, some curls and some weights. I could feel my blood pumping and testosterone rising. I love this feeling after the gym. I feel in control of my life. Back upstairs, I had a quick shower. I gazed at the closet. Grey, black or navy suit? I checked my calendar. There was a Global Directors' meeting but it was a video conference. I went with slacks and a blazer instead. In the kitchen, I grabbed the sandwich I'd made the night before for lunch. There'll be no time to eat out today. My calendar was packed. I grabbed my briefcase and car keys and headed for the door. Then turned back to throw a
~~~

power bar and energy drink in my briefcase. 6:45am. If traffic was in my favor, I'd have just enough time to stop by Starbucks for my morning coffee en route to make the 7:17am train to Union station from the Oakville Go station.

Traffic was okay. But when I pulled into the Starbucks drive-through I got concerned. The line-up of cars was too long. I swung to go into the parking lot instead. I cut a guy off with my quick swerve. He gave me a finger and yelled profanities. I ignored him. I figured no one had had their coffee yet. The line-up inside was not as bad as outside. I sized up the baristas and figured they were moving people through at 40 seconds on average. That was 3 people every 2 minutes. I was 9th in line. I glanced at my watch again. 7:00am. I could spare 6 minutes for my coffee. The Go train was just across the street.

I tried to stop tapping my foot anxiously as I waited in line. Such a painfully long wait this was. I distracted myself by watching people, taking in our collective impatience. People were glancing at their watches every 3 seconds. The tattooed guy who looked like a truck driver was mumbling under his breath. The goth girl was examining her black nails and trying not to look bored at looking bored. The other black guy in a suit caught my eye and acknowledged me with a nod. I tried to say hey to the kid with his cap turned backwards and his pants halfway down his legs. He studiously ignored me. I wondered what his story was. 7:06am. The girl in front of me was taking longer than her 40 seconds. She obviously was not a regular and was asking for an explanation of everything.

Crap!

There needs to be a Starbucks for Newbies line where they do translation.

I really need to download the Starbucks order app.

Gonna do it on the train so I can order from home tomorrow on my way in.

I was just about to leave when the other barista called me over. I tried not to stare as I ordered my straight-up grande latte. She was stunning. Caramel-colored, she was fresh-faced with no make-up, only lip gloss. I wondered if that's why I noticed her. I thought of telling her she was beautiful but instead asked how long she'd worked there since I'd never seen her before. She's new here she said as she wrote my order on the cup - the hours work better for her college schedule. "Have a nice day sir," she said. I hesitated, then saw that it was almost 7:10am and heard the person behind me breathing impatiently. I flashed an appreciative smile at the stunning barista and headed out. I made it across the street, parked somewhat crookedly and was standing on the platform at precisely 7:16 as the train rolled in.

I felt pleased to have made the train as I sat down. I leaned back and closed my eyes, letting myself settle from the rush of the drive and Starbucks expedition. When I opened my eyes, the old lady across from me was staring.

"You're very handsome!" She said with a toothless grin

I smiled back politely and non-committally, feeling awkward. I was suddenly glad I hadn't told the Starbucks barista she was beautiful.

I sipped my coffee and pulled out my iPhone to start checking work messages. 117 unread emails. I clicked on the last unread message from yesterday at 9pm. I regretted the decision to read my email by the time I'd finished the first one.

~~~

By the time the train pulled into Union station, I'd deleted a bunch of junk email and mass emails that I was copied on and had quickly gone through about 30 of the rest. I got off and joined the flow of people walking briskly to their various offices. Downtown Toronto always felt like a mimic of New York City to me. Everyone rushing
~~~

about in swirls of colors and speed.

Everyone's rushing through their lives!

What's the point?

I was surprised by the thought. I suddenly had an eerie sense of seeing a kaleidoscope of people in my mind's eye, spinning along aimlessly back and forth, to the gym, from Starbucks, to the Go train, and in and out of my revolving doors at the Royal City Tower as I walked in. The pretty girl from Starbucks stood out in the sea of faces. I shook my head and had more coffee.

I got to my office, making sure to say hi to our assistant, Helen, on the way in. She was nice and it helped me to have her on my side. There's a message for you from Sanya in marketing, she said. They sent you an email this morning but haven't heard back. They're shooting a new ad for the African Mines Company and they want you to be the narrator. I grimaced. I was getting weary of being the poster boy for all things Africa and for being on the roster of options for diversity shoots. I might recommend that they use an actual model or actor next time so I can stick with business and legal issues.

I dug into the piles of documents waiting for responses on my desk. A recommendation here. A signature there. I read a few more emails. I had an hour to go before my 11:00am meeting and so much more to wade through. My gym and coffee routine usually had me on a high at this time of the morning but I felt dull today. I ruffled through my briefcase for my power bar, ripped it open and took a bite. I did a few more emails and got up to head to the men's. Helen looked up and asked:

"Are you ok, Mr. Mansaray?"

"Yeah," I said and continued on.

I stood in front of the urinal and took a piss, letting out gas at the same time and enjoying the relief and momentary stillness. I went over to wash my hands. I stared at my reflection. Aunty Amie stared back.

I had only fleetingly thought of the news this morning in the shower and had not given it another thought until now. I was the exact reflection of her. Rounded head. Narrow eyes, a nose that couldn't decide if it wanted to be flat or full, a strong jawline, slightly heavyset, shiny dark chocolate skin. When I was a boy, the older girls in our compound used to put a head wrap on me and marvel at how much I looked like Aunty Amie. She always had a headwrap on, and I could see thick afro pigtails that refused to stay straight and coiled upwards under her headwrap.

You look exactly like her! They'd squeal.

And I'd always cry. I did not want to look like Aunty Amie. I did not like her.

And as if the gods were goading me, the last time I travelled home, I could not help but admit that I did indeed look exactly like her. I'd started going bald in my early thirties and shaved my head. Aunty Amie had also shaved her head. She was too old to fuss with hair, she'd said. She enjoyed the feeling of water on her head in the heat. She still wore her headwraps for weddings and events but mostly stayed all day with her very shiny bald head in my dad's compound where she lived.

I washed my face, as if to wash off her image in it. I felt suddenly tired. She was no more, so that meant only I bore this resemblance in the world. My father, her brother, apparently looked exactly like their mother who had some Fulani in her. They couldn't look more opposite. He was light-skinned, narrow-featured and narrow limbed. Apparently, the only thing Aunty Amie had inherited from NaNa, was her thick hair. Otherwise, she and I looked exactly like Grandpa Mansaray. I resented being responsible to now hold their resemblance in the world.

I went back to my desk and headed to my 11:00am meeting.

~~~

The Asia-Pacific Director was presenting. I had a mild headache. I was last on the agenda to present for North America - East Coast. My mind drifted off to Aunty Amie.

I did not like Aunty Amie growing up because I knew Aunty Amie did not like me. I remember as a child being scared of her. She was this formidable force that swooped in and transformed everything. When she showed-up from the Provinces, Mama seemed to shrink away and Papa became like the children we had read about in the book at school - The Pied Piper of Hamelin. Before she arrived, I'd be allowed to play around Papa, running with the other boys in our compound, playing soccer or creating toys out of scraps. Whenever she arrived, the air became heavy. She'd say - this boy is too loud! and Papa will say, Sam, be quiet! She'd say, I found this boy misbehaving in the front yard with the street boys! He should be spanked. And Papa would spank me without asking. Nothing went well when Aunty Amie was around. So, I had learnt like Mama, to transform into a meek boy, sucked of all juice like a well-squeezed orange. The only time I heard Aunty Amie laugh, was usually after she had succeeded to drive everyone away and had Papa all to herself. They'd sit on the balcony talking and laughing and any of us in the household would only be summoned to tend to their needs.

I couldn't figure out why Aunty Amie didn't like me or Mama, until one day when Mama was away on a trip. She had a USAID contract to go around the country doing health sensitizations and facilitating dialogues for women. My mom's cousin, Fatu was staying with us to help Papa with me. The day I came from school and saw Aunty Amie on the balcony with Papa, I was petrified! Fatu had left me at the side gate to go in and ran off to the market to buy
~~~

ingredients to prepare the evening meal. They were in deep conversation but I knew something was wrong because Aunty Amie wasn't talking and laughing like she usually did when she had Papa to herself. I slithered to the back without saying hi to either of them. It was bad enough when Mama was around. I felt completely unprotected without her home.

I quietly changed and stayed in my room. But I was hungry, so I snuck into the kitchen. I found some plantains and akara on the counter and grabbed a couple. On my way back to my room, my curiosity got the best of me. Heart pumping in my chest, I inched close to the open balcony window and quietly crouched down behind a chair. I heard Aunty Amie saying:

"I don't know why you won't listen to me! Heed my words! You know what they say 'one pikin not to pikin, na eg!'"

One child isn't a child, it's just an egg!

"Take a second wife! Or send this woman away and remarry if taking a second wife is so abhorrent to you!"

"Sister, I will not agree with you or relent on this. I will not leave my wife or remarry. God has blessed us with a son and if he's the only child we will have, then so be it."

I didn't wait to hear more.

I never told Mama what I had heard. I realized then that she probably knew why Aunty Amie didn't like her. My child's mind couldn't quite understand why she would dislike me because I was an only child. But since that day I decided that I would do well. I would make my parents proud. And I will never like Aunty Amie.

~~~

North America, Pacific Northwest was up. That meant, I was next. I tried to listen to my colleague, but I was finding it hard to focus. I
~~~

went to the coffee station using the short walk to stretch and refocus. I came back and stood behind my chair listening to the update. But my mind kept drifting to that last time I saw Aunty Amie. I'd gone home for the Christmas holidays. I hadn't been back for about 7 years at that point although I'd seen my parents quite a bit. They had come to Toronto for my Masters graduation and had been to the U.S. for business or conferences after that. Whenever they were on the East Coast, I'd drive over to the Washington DC area where they typically stayed with our relatives to see them. But that year, we decided I should go home for Christmas because I hadn't been back in 7 years. It was a great time of reunion with old friends I grew up with in the capital Freetown and with friends and family I visited in the Provinces. We had all grown-up and changed - some more than others. My biggest surprise though was Aunty Amie.

As an adult, my dislike for Aunty Amie had dulled to a faint indifference. I wasn't actively mad at her. She just didn't matter to me. I didn't think to ask after her. When my mom mentioned that she was moving into our Freetown compound, I was alarmed!

"How will you handle that Mama?" I asked with concern.

She'd laughed, saying:

"Aunty Amie has made her peace with me. She's not who she used to be." I didn't understand what that meant until I saw her.

When I arrived home, I was flooded with the usual screams and greetings. I greeted the whole household and went to do rounds in the neighborhood. When I came back, Aunty Amie was waiting at the gate for me. She stood there, stooped over a walking stick. I waited for her to straighten up. I waited for the stick to be raised over her head and for the scolding to start. We stood silently watching each other. It was then I noticed the years etched into her face as our perfect resemblance dawned on me. It was also then I realized that the years had shrunk her or that I had outgrown her. Suddenly, I heard a wail rise sharply into the air. I couldn't tell if Aunty Amie was shedding tears of joy, or pain, or relief. All I remember is that she was suddenly in my arms, making a pitiful sound repeating over and over again: "My father and my son! My father and my son!" I was confused by my sudden urge to protect her as it dawned on me how alone this woman was but for us. I'd never paused or stopped to think about the fact that she had been widowed at a very young age, had never remarried and had no children. The formidable Aunty Amie had lost her aura and I wasn't sure what to make of it.

The rest of the vacation, Aunty Amie cried every single time she laid eyes on me. Mama felt the need to keep explaining and admonishing: She is overwhelmed. She's an old woman now. She's your only aunt. You should make peace with her. I remained indifferent. I did see a glimpse of the old Aunty Amie briefly. One day I was asleep and was awoken by her screaming voice. I raced outside, my heart beating a little faster than usual at the memories her screaming voice evoked. What was all the commotion?! One of the neighborhood boys had used his rubber slingshot to hit Aunty Amie's bald head with a rolled-up piece of paper. She caught the boy and was giving him a thorough thrashing with her walking stick. I rescued him, reprimanded him and sent him on his way.

For the first time, Aunty Amie and I laughed together afterwards. I examined the spot where she'd taken the hit. It's okay she said, it'll be fine. I just needed to teach him a lesson. We talked for a while. She told me stories of her own childhood with my dad. She shared with me what my grandparents were like. How she had longed for children of her own. How my other uncles and aunties had died of a strange fever outbreak when they were young leaving only her and a younger Papa and how she had raised him protectively, scared of losing him too. She looked at me, her eyes boring my soul. You are a man now she said. You carry our name, image and bloodline. Please, hurry and marry. Promise you will find a girl and bear us some children. You are our only child, our only hope.

I was stunned by the forceful pull of her words. My instant desire to please her sickened me. I had recoiled from her. I would not marry on Aunty Amie's command. I would not succumb to her spell like Papa used to.

After our talk, I stayed distant from her for the rest of the holidays. When I left, she was standing at the gate where she greeted me. I could hear her wailing until we were out of earshot heading to the helicopter for the short flight to Lungi airport.

"Samuel?"

"Samuel?"

"You're up now...you okay?"

Our Vice President's voice jolted me back.

"Yes, my apologies. Here's the update on North America - East Coast." Our numbers are better than last weeks'…." I droned on through the numbers and slides in the file Helen had handed me.

~~~

The rest of the day was a blur. I remember having my energy drink after the Global Director's meeting and then headed into another 3-hour meeting with my team. At 5:30pm, as our team meeting ended, I noticed I now had 288 emails. I also realized I had to race out to make it to MoneyGram in the Shoppers Drug Mart around the corner before they closed. Papa had expected me to send the money earlier in the day so he'd have it by evening his time. I decided I'll wake up to call him first thing in the morning his time with the details. If only he'd just use text messages!

I was about to bolt to do the money transfer when Pravin intercepted me. Pravin grew up in India and had moved to Toronto from Dubai 2 years earlier. He'd also lived in Sudan, Rwanda and The Democratic Republic of Congo. We got along, often sharing our
~~~

third-world-problems and experiences with each other.

"Wanna go for drinks, man? You look a bit stressed today -- what's happening?"

"No man, I'm ok. Just need to go send some cash home. My aunt, my dad's only sister died. Got the call at 3:00am."

"Sorry to hear it - were you gonna go send the cash now - don't tell me you're going to MoneyGram or Western Union?! I can help you"

"What you mean?"

"My uncle, the one who visited last year from Dubai…."

"Yeah, I remember him…"

"Yeah - he started doing money transfer to Africa. Said he has a guy in Ghana and Sierra Leone - meant to tell you, man. Look, it's going to 6pm here so almost 5am in Dubai. My uncle will be up in an hour. You can send him the message on his app. You email the money transfer to him. He'll deposit in his Canadian account and send you confirmation and codes. Then he texts his guy in Sierra Leone and your Pa can pick up in the morning his time."

"Seriously, man. That'll be so fresh. You guys got yourself a customer!"

Within the hour, I'd gone on the app and made my transaction. By 7:30pm, I was down to 150 emails and my phone had beeped with confirmations and codes from Pravin's uncle. I decided to call it a day.

What's the point of these 12-hour days anyway?

The kaleidoscope images swirled through my mind again. The stunning barista was still there, but this time Aunty Amie's face was also in the crowds, walking along with me.

~~~

I decided to stay downtown and go for drinks. I'd missed the last Go train back anyway and would have to cab or get a ride to the station to pick my car. I should sell my place and move into the city, I thought. But I loved my place in Oakville. I'd bought it when I worked in Mississauga and didn't want to give it up to rent in the city. Too bad there was no one and nothing waiting at home for me. Not even a dog. Maybe I should get one. I wondered what it would be like to go home to a wife and kids. I'd always brushed the thought aside. Maybe it was time to think about it. I'd be 40 in three months. Poor Aunty Amie never got her wish. I tried to imagine how she would have reacted if I'd gone home to marry a bride. Probably would have been the best gift I could ever have given her. Too late for that now.

I headed for O! lounge in the Yonge-Dundas square area - Toronto's Times Square. A couple of my buddies were there. Some had dates with them and others didn't. It didn't matter. It was NBA season and we were all glued to the Rockets vs. Clippers game in the Western Conference playoffs. I wasn't sure if I'd watch till the end though. We had some global executives visiting tomorrow and I needed to be on my A-game. I decided to have a few more drinks and then head out. I needed one and looked around for the bartenders. I saw what looked like a shift change happening as the game went to commercials. I took my phone to download the Starbucks app, then hesitated - having the app might mean I won't get to see the stunning barista. I lifted my head and her dazzling smile greeted me from across the bar:

"Hey Starbucks customer from this morning, what drink can I get you?"

I felt myself get as tongue-tied as I was when I had my first crush on Kadijah when I was 9.
~~~

I heard my voice say: “What’s your name?”

“Amina,” She replied.

7 THE CONFERENCE

The aged world-renowned professor that was skyped into the conference was saying, in the voice of quiet authority that only those who have read many books and lived very long can have: "we will not change our world until we recognize that we cannot exist in silos and until we invite understandings from all over the world – until we make gatherings like this truly multicultural! Until we stop trying to 'help' those we think to be helpless. That's like giving sugar to a diabetic! We need to get in relationship with people, learn from each other and learn again to truly relate by how we love, which we all instinctively know by the micro-affirmations we receive. That's what the theory of social relatedness is really about!"

All around Sameliza, heads were bobbing as conference delegates vigorously agreed. The Professor was preaching to the converted. This was a room full of academics, social activists, entrepreneurs and change consultants. People from all over the globe who had gathered in South Africa to talk about changing the world through positivity, to share ideas and to inspire one another. The professor's words were being drunk down like another glass of hard liquor to alcoholics at the party with an open bar, each glass making them happier than before.

But Sameliza wanted to cry. *I'm in dissonance* she thought, as she felt the insides of her gut knotting. She experienced what seemed like a small column of pain from her chest rise through her and lodge itself behind her eyes. Her temples started throbbing. She thought: *Am I insane? Can no one else see what I see?* She scanned the room again. Over the sea of bobbing heads, she spotted the Kenya woman she'd met at registration. They had gravitated to each other like magnets.

"Allo," the Kenyan woman said.

"My name is Njoki. What is yours? Sameliza?! That's an interesting name." Sameliza had smiled noncommittally, not about to explain her name.

Njoki had shared that she worked for an NGO that gets homeless children off the street. She was getting burnt out and had come here for inspiration and to find community.

"Please, let us meet again eh. The topics of the speakers look good but I also want to meet other Africans who we'd be able to share challenges and ideas with."

Sameliza had promised to find Njoki later.

She scanned the room again and she spotted the black American woman, LaShondra. She wore her hair in dreadlocks and had also approached Sameliza in the lobby –

"Sista girl, where you from?!"

"Sierra Leone," Sameliza replied.

"Ah," LaShondra had said, "I'm so happy to be here! Here in the Motherland. My doctoral dissertation was about *African-American Identities in relation to the African continent.*"

Sameliza had started to drown LaShondra out. She seemed like a nice lady, but Sameliza sensed she was heading for the inevitable conversation about what growing up in Africa had been like and she wasn't in the mood to start talking about that either. How could she even begin to explain that growing up in Sierra Leone had simply meant growing up, not growing up black? The last time she had tried to explain that to a black American girl while on vacation to the States, the girl had ended up yelling at her:

"You are a damn elite African! Your ancestors sold us! How dare you say you don't identify as Black American! Let me break it to you African girl – you are in American now and here, you are as black as all of us slave descendants!"

Sameliza had managed to recover enough from the shock to say calmly:

"Actually, my name is a combination of Samuel and Elizabeth. Those are my parents' names. My family name is Caulker. I hope you caught those are Anglo-Saxon names and other than my middle name, Kehinde to remind me of my African-ness, are wholly foreign. That means we are Creole and are descendants of freed slaves who chose to go back to Africa – after a slave master changed our names. And even if I wasn't a Creole who shares your history, even if I was a non-Creole Sierra Leonean whose descendants may or may not have been a part of the trade, and who may themselves have lost descendants to the trade, what gives you the right to discount mine and others' experiences just because it isn't the same as yours? You should try reading *Book of Negroes* - that might help you start to understand the other part of your history." She had walked away, leaving the girl in stunned silence.

Sameliza had made small talk with LaShondra, trying to politely extricate herself. But LaShondra continued: "you have no idea how blessed you are to know where you come from, where your roots are. I'd give anything to know. It's a hard reality to live with but I promised myself long time ago I just gatta keep on living the life I've been blessed with. Yessir I just gatta keep on living."

A wave of sadness had swept over Sameliza. Sadness for the histories that followed and trapped them all, sadness for the generational impact of social injustice and oppression. It's the reason she was at this conference. She was a psychologist working in post-war Sierra Leone, and had quickly realized that the post-traumatic development of the nation required more than individual rehabilitation, it required social transformation and Sameliza was looking for her role in that.

Just as she had been about to respond, from a more gracious place than she originally intended, Sara had showed up saying:

"Hey Sammy, we must go in now – you are all registered, isn't it?"

Sara, her South African friend of 15 years, her roommate in university in Vancouver, Canada. She was the white girlfriend every black girl should have. Sameliza bade farewell to LaShondra as she rushed off after Sara, smiling as she thought, *she's always been speedy, decisive* and recalling the first time they met. It had been a context not unlike the present, in the registration and orientation hall of their university. It was full, vibrant and buzzing with new students eager to start university, mostly tantalized by the thought that they had their freedom to be adults, live on campus, do whatever they wished between classes and party all night. The din of conversation was abuzz with that anticipatory exaggeration that seemed to characterize all young people's conversations in Canada and the US. Every conversation started with "Oh my God!" and ended with "isn't that AWESOME? [Canadian]" or "isn't that AMAZING?" [American]. The listener responded as if by robotic rote "OMG that's AMAZING!" or "totally AWESOME!" The response was always the same, even when the only thing amazing or awesome about the conversation was how empty it all was.

Straight from Sierra Leone, Sameliza had been standing in stunned silence, overwhelmed by it all. She was used to the direct and realist abruptness of Sierra Leoneans and most West Africans. So, as she stood eavesdropping in the registration line for campus residents, she kept thinking, *why won't anyone tell the truth! That's not amazing, that's a stupid idea. No Sir, ah ah, telling the girl you just met that you think she's your wife is not AWESOME! It might get you slapped!* Then, into her monologue arrived matter-of-fact Sara. She'd seemed to just appear beside Sameliza and whispered loud enough for only Sameliza to hear:

"Can you believe this stupidity – 'Oh my God!' 'Oh my God!'" she said in her mimicry voice, "I'm seriously gonna lose it any minute now and knock someone's head!"

Sameliza had laughed out loud – her boisterous, full laugh ringing out and making heads turn. It was the laughter of relief and instant kinship. They'd sized each other up, Sameliza noticing Sara's sensible face – pretty dark eyes set in square features topped with dark long hair. There was something very knowing, yet safe about Sara. Sameliza would come to learn it was that she could call things as they are and laugh at herself and others in that dry witty way that anchored everyone, without rescuing or alienating anyone. She had a way of asking just the question to crack open people's thinking, without seeming judgmental.

Sara had said: "I like your braids. You're pretty." The latter, again stated as a matter of fact, as she took in Sameliza's micro braids, slight frame, dark chocolate skin and small slanty eyes set above high cheekbones.

"Do you have a roommate yet?" When Sameliza shook her head no, she'd extended her hand -

"Wanna be roomies." They'd introduced themselves and Sara said: "Sameliza? What kind of name is that?!"

"Long story, but basically Sierra Leonean parents are fond of naming their children with made-up combinations of their own, even when the name does sound made-up and let's just say not necessarily nice.

For me, it's always been a great conversation starter."

They'd been besties since and their friends called them The Sisters, since they introduced themselves like that. Right from the start they had planned their return to their respective African homes after university, simultaneously laughing and getting infuriated by the "insanely ignorant," as Sara called them, questions and situations they'd run into. Like when students would say "OMG you are both from Africa!" and then turn to Sara, cutting Sameliza out of the conversation and say something along the lines of "how come you grew up there? That's so cool! Were there always animals and stuff? I guess it's better that you are here now with the war in Africa, eh?" And ultimately, they would tease each other mercilessly when they too, started finding everything "AWESOME!"

Ten years after their meeting was their first trip together to South Africa, when they were both returning home. Sameliza spent a month with Sara and her family before heading to Sierra Leone. Sara had said flatly before they left:

"You need to know that it is 10 years after apartheid but there is still voluntary segregation and change is slow. My family lives in an all-white neighborhood outside Joburg, eat at all-white restaurants, hang-out with all-white friends and go to an all-white church. My parents were anti-apartheid but I have no guarantee that we won't run into people who might make racist or classist comments. My parents tell me their close friend Jan is always coming around complaining about blacks taking over the country and how hard it is for whites to find jobs now because of affirmative action. If we want to hang out with sistas we'll have to ask my one black friend from growing up during apartheid – our housekeeper Happy's daughter. Thembi is off studying but I can track her down and we can go into Soweto or Maboneng with her or something, but we sure won't be going on our own! Think you can handle all that?"

"I can handle most anything when I am with you Sara!" Sameliza had replied with a chuckle.

Sameliza had thought that her first encounter with South Africa would prepare her for this one. She'd been overwhelmed then with the ease with which dialogue turned to race, what it meant to be black, white, Indian or colored in South Africa and the subtle and not so subtle inferences to her being an even different category of a "black African from the rest of Africa." She had gone in and out of being overwhelmed as a West African who'd grown up without being immersed in racial distinctions. While she and Sara had agreed Canada wasn't as racially tolerant as it liked to claim, Canadian dialogue on race was often subtler, inferred indirectly and below the line. Sameliza had been swept up in the American racial dialogue and politics with other black and African students for sure, but living North of the US had provided some insulation from it all. South Africans' open dialogue on race, apartheid and truth and reconciliation had been both refreshing and overwhelming.

And now, five more years after her first visit, at this conference, Sameliza was surprised by the conflicting feelings sweeping through her - a jumble of sadness, anger and fatigue from it all. Sara turned to Sameliza who was still scanning the room and said in the same tone of quiet disbelief she'd had in that campus registration line all those years ago.

"Shit! It's 2014, 20 years after the end of apartheid and we are still slow to learn. I think I met 5 other South Africans earlier – all white - plus the folks you met and the Indian delegation from Dubai, I bet there are no more than 30 non-whites, non-westerners here of the 300 delegates. Ten percent or less! I mean, how much did the conference registration cost?! This is the hallmark of western privilege in this room – 'let's go to AFRICA and help the poor people there while we have fun!' The veil of privilege is so finely spread, they can't even catch the colonial irony. This room isn't even representative of South Africa, let alone multicultural or the world!

Let's gather like this if we must, but let's call it what it is - not a 'world' conference. If it's for the world, the world must be here! It is again 250 westerners gathered to talk about what must happen in the world. This has to change."

Sameliza could tell Sara was mad because she said shit. It was the only swear word she ever used and only in extreme circumstances in her view. Somewhere in her, despite her outspoken nature, she was still a good Afrikaner girl who didn't swear. Her matter-of-fact approach to life usually kept her grounded. Perhaps it was because this was happening in South Africa, the rainbow nation, her home, where they had started leading the way for the world in these issues and now seemed to be slowing down in the progress they had made.

Sameliza said "Add eastern wealth to your white privilege. You did mention Dubai and I helped the Chinese delegation find their way and register this morning!"

Sara smiled in spite of herself. "The balance of power is still in the western privilege, at least in this room."

Sameliza paused, then responded: "are we just being self-righteous?"

Sara retorted: "Someone better be and call it, coz there sure isn't going to be any opposing views in this crowd! Blind spots are blind spots. We all have them when we don't know what we don't know. We all need to listen and learn from each other more!"

After the plenary, they headed out to find their first breakout workshop. They had decided to go to the same one on *Leading Social Change*. Out in the hallway, they were finding their way there when she heard someone calling out "Dr. Caulker!" Sameliza swung around. A smiling woman with short blond hair approached her.

"Dr. Caulker I just wanted to introduce myself. My name is Heidi. I work with African refugee youth in Spain and with both Israeli and Palestinian children who've been traumatized in the Gaza area and I am really looking forward to hearing about your work on the *Impact of Social Trauma and the possibility of Posttraumatic Growth* later today."

"oh…sh…right!" Sameliza said, thinking - *my turn to say shit.* She had forgotten she was on a panel in the last session before the conference closed.

"Thank you" She managed. And then to distract herself from her rising panic, she said "Heidi? And you work in Spain and the Middle East?"

Yes, she laughed. I was born in Germany but grew up in the Middle East. My parents volunteered there in various post-conflict areas – Peace Corps. In Spain, I work with an organization offering psychosocial support to immigrants and refugees, helping them job search and such."

"Impressive" Sameliza said. "I was also born in Germany but my family left when I was 2 for Sierra Leone."

"Oh funny! I just met another lady who was born in Germany in the ladies' room! What a coincidence – the Germans have no idea the brain drain they have experienced," she said with a laugh as big as Sameliza's. "Although it isn't nearly the same as what is happening for African countries. I really hope we can talk more later."

"Yes." Sameliza said. "Perhaps we can sit together at the closing gala after my talk, then we can share more ideas from our work?"

Sameliza watched her walked away. There was something very likeable about her. She was tall and slightly ungainly in her walk and yet was very sure-footed about herself. Sameliza smiled, suddenly encouraged as she headed to the first session. She found Sara as she walked into the room, surrounded by a group of men. Sameliza inched forward to join them – it sounded like they were all change consultants working in profit, non-profit and social entrepreneurship. They were talking about the challenges of their work. The conversation seemed to have revived Sara.

Just then the session started. The speakers introduced themselves and started into the description of their work, which turned out to be a social change model researched in the United States that was being tested with local women in Uganda. The speakers were talking about the challenges they were having with data collection and accountability to the outcomes of the program. The women seemed to engage well in the community dialogues with their peers, but not with the other aspects of the program. They turned it to the room to ask for ideas.

Sara piped up: "I recently worked with a women's group in South Africa who wanted to move their community from impoverished to self-sustaining. When I arrived, I talked about all the corporate partners we could get involved and the women looked at me and said: 'please, if people are coming to help, they must help us on our terms. Please tell them not to come to fix us, we are not broken; not to adopt us, we are not pets; not to give us junk/hand me downs – we do not want charity; and not to tell us what to do, rather to learn with us, because we are not stupid.'[2] That encounter has stayed with me and shifted how I work in social change. I am wondering, what dialogue have you had with the women about what they want? How would your program rate across these four criteria from the South African women?"

The speakers were taken aback, red in the face at first, but gradually engaged the ideas as the room erupted into lively dialogue about the issues raised by Sara. By the end of the session, one of the men said "wow, maybe we have gone about this all wrong. We'd fail on all those criteria in the eyes of the South African women and that's probably what's going on for the Ugandan women!"

---

[2] Real comment made by Louise Van Rhyn in a talk about her work with Partners4Possibility in South Africa, July 2014.

Good old Sara has done it again, I thought as I grinned at her. She winked back, saying "dassai" Afrikaans lingo for "that's it!"

That session gave Sameliza the wind she needed in her sails for her panel. She felt grounded and clear as she started her talk: "When we work with people who have experienced social trauma, what is our story of them? What assumptions do we start with? What potential do we see for our clients? Do we start from a place of pity or from a place of connected humanity?..." As Sameliza addressed the audience, she was met by Sara's and Heidi's beaming faces. Some other faces beamed liked theirs and still others wore the intensely puzzled look of those being asked questions they had never considered. Sameliza knew it was going well. The loud applause at the end confirmed her hunch. During the question period, a man who sounded Dutch, said: "Dr. Caulker, you are well-spoken and educated, compared to most of ze Afrikans we see in Europa. Ze ways of working you suggest, do they really work wiz ze less educated and impoverished Afrikans?"

Sameliza serenely asked: "where are you from, Sir?"

"The Netherlands" he replied.

"Sir, would you work with the poor and impoverished in The Netherlands as human equals or as less intelligent, incapable human beings? If you wouldn't do so for the poor and impoverished in The Netherlands, there is no reason to think or suggest it must be so for people of African descent. People are people, deserving of respect and dignity. Africans are no less intelligent than others or incapable of finding their own solutions simply because we have struggled with educational and wealth inequities in the global picture. You do not need a western education to answer the question: 'what do I want for my own life now?'" The room erupted in applause again and into deep dialogue about ways in which people working in the social sector can inadvertently dehumanize others.

The panel ended with an Indian woman, Indira, talking about *Indian Women Rising.* Indira had caramel-colored skin. She was big boned and full-bodied with perfectly straight, long, black hair. She looked beautiful as she spoke, oozing with self-assurance and confidence, captivating the room. Her Indian accent was laced with a non-pretentious British one, indicating she had spent years studying in the UK. She was the kind of woman less self-assured women loved to hate, because they were both drawn to her and repelled by her presence, as she inadvertently reminded them of the confidence they lacked.

It was a refreshing and provocative ending for Sameliza and Sara as Indira candidly talked about negotiating her identity as an educated woman in a patriarchal society, who also loved the traditional roles easily ascribed to her as wife and mother. Indira was CEO of one of the fastest growing telecom companies in India, with a dream of providing access to mobile technologies to the poorest, most disadvantaged communities in India. She was making it happen in spite of major setbacks, simply by building relationship and communities. She talked about coaching other women and Sara and Sameliza both said simultaneously, "I want her to coach me!" Both Sara and Sameliza were in relationships that were getting serious and they'd spent sleepless nights talking to each other about how to be married and not lose themselves.

At the closing ceremony, Sara and Sameliza were joined at their table by Indira and her husband who was beaming ear-to-ear, proud of his wife. Heidi and Njoki also joined, along with two Canadian men who were thrilled that Sameliza and Sara had lived and studied in Canada and were clearly open to a night of flirting. One of the co-presenters for the closing talk was a woman named Miatta Goma. She was a Liberian woman, who had been part of the Liberian Women's movement that ended the war there and for which Leymah Gboweh won the Nobel Peace Prize. Miatta's resume was a litany of work with all the international and world agencies, where she advocated for reducing financial aid to African countries and increasing capacity for African grown solutions to African problems. And she advocated that eloquently now. Her co-presenter was a Brazilian man who spoke of advocating and working in the resistance movements across Latin America, fueled by philosophies of Paulo Freire's *conscientization* - engaging people in critical dialogue about the oppressive structures that impact them, and so creating the possibility of social transformation through social action.

Sameliza found herself hooting and hollering in agreement as the two spoke, and especially when Miatta did. Her table and a few others were like cheerleaders in a church congregation, shouting, chuckling and saying Amen in agreement to the ideas. She noticed that the loudest cheers were coming from the few tables that represented global diversity in the room. Suddenly, she had a realization. She was proud of Miatta, just as she had been proud of Indira earlier, and as she was to be sitting with Heidi, Sara and Njoki at this table with the Canadian men and the Indian husband. She was proud, because they were ambassadors of the untold stories they represented and by the challenge they presented in their being and essence. All of them, had learnt the art of living and slipping in and out of all the worlds they represented seamlessly, without wanting to be less of one or the other.

The western-educated African women, the European working in the middle east, the Indian wife and mother, The Afrikaner woman, the Kenyan woman who cared less about her accent and more about the children she served, the Canadian men, unafraid to join the table of 'others,' the Indian man who beamed at his CEO wife. In that moment, Sameliza realized, that it was the ease with which they lived in their worlds, wholeheartedly and realistically, that made a difference. They were present to each world, such that they were not seen, other than by the most prejudiced, as a "sell-out" in the eyes of their own communities or an "other" in the eyes of other peoples. This was the way of the new world.

She also felt ashamed, as she realized she had not felt this way about the Khoi San and Zulu leaders who had opened the conference. Then, it was the bobbing heads of westerners who'd been cheering when the men came out in their traditional garb and spoke through a translator. Sameliza had found it irritating, even though she understood the need to preserve culture and language. It had seemed to her like the parade of the indigenous, being brought out for the Westerners to admire, and reinforcing the stereotype of Africa as a place of an exotic, indigenous peoples only. She was all the more angered, because she knew the speakers were both professors of African history at the University of South Africa (UNISA) and very capable of speaking in the language the audience would understand as well as their own languages, and could translate for themselves.

The closing ceremony speakers were ending and the dance troop of entertainers came out, all South African men, bare-chested and singing in that unmistakably, powerfully melodious Sound African sound, singing *Nkosi sikelel' iAfrika* and a mixture of traditional and contemporary songs to a band and drums. Our table moved and swayed between conversations, enjoying the music. The room erupted as a women Sameliza had chatted with earlier ran up to dance with the men. Sameliza had noticed her because she was extremely pale, a paleness that was accentuated by very dark hair and bright red lipstick that made her stand out among the other women. Now, the pale lady gyrated, hollered and swayed slightly off-beat until she started sweating even though it was winter in South Africa.

Sameliza, unable to help herself blurted out:

"Man! She looks like she's about to have an orgasm!"

She surprised herself by instantly looking apologetically at Indira's husband, relieved when he and everyone at the table started laughing.

"Glad you said it! I was thinking it but didn't dare say it in this crowd in case one of you labelled me sexist!" said one of the Canadian guys.

The black American woman with dreadlocks ran over to their table, with an exaggerated "can I join y'all! Y'all are having way too much fun up in here! Can you believe this lady?!"

Later, as Sameliza left the party, jumping into the uber car for her ride to the Oliver Tambo airport, the uber driver took her bags, then taking her in said: "You look happy – must have been a great party?" "Yes," Sameliza responded, her smile broadening – "It was a great conference and party – there is hope."

8 STANDING IN THE RAIN

Maya's hands were flying on the keyboard as she typed furiously.

Another damn email to respond to. She just wanted to go home. She used to love her job as Corporate Communications Director at Xtron. She was realizing lately that she was losing patience for all the organizational politics surrounding her words. An email response after a bulletin release was never a simple thing. They were publicly traded and her words were considered to be officially from the CEO and could send shareholders screaming.

Unfortunately, the new version will not be released…

She backspaced furiously, annoyed with herself. She was tired and hungry but even so, who started a response to a stakeholder with unfortunately!

The new version of Mecatron will be released on July 15, 2015. This will allow us to fully integrate all the requirements requested by users in the previous engagement process…

There - that's better, she thought. She tapped her heels impatiently on the floor as her fingers kept flying across the keyboard. She was aware of the brightness streaming through the windows and willed herself to stay focused. It was a beautiful summer day in Victoria, BC and she just wanted to get out and go enjoy the evening. They should go out for dinner at the pier or maybe they should drive out to Sidney for a change. She felt like sushi. Then they could go for gelato and take a leisurely walk after. She should call Emmanuel and tell him that's the plan for tonight. She'll wear the new multi-colored sundress she just bought.

Focus, focus, she thought. She was stuck on how to close. Could she use sincerely and not sound blatantly insincere? The truth was that they had messed up the requirements and left testing too late. By the time they found the glitches, there was no way they'd make the original release date.

Buzzzzzzz

She ignored her ringing phone.

Thank you for continuing to partner with us as we extend the promotion events leading up to the new release date

With Thanks,

Maya Akinola

Buzzzzzzz

She hit enter and continued to ignore the phone as she packed up quickly. She threw her keys and sunglasses in her purse as she wiggled her feet back into her heels under her desk. Her phone had stopped ringing.

Buzzzzzzz!

Oh man! She checked the call display. She smiled as she answered the call, pushing back her chair and heading for the door.

"Hey Yema! How are you my potho sister?" Maya said.

"Hey my blasian sister!" Yema responded.

They laughed in unison, their playful name calling, a signal of their bond that had grown over their shared heritage. Maya's dad was from Ghana and her mom was from the Philippines. She had told Yema once that blasian was the term in her community for black-Asians. Yema in return, had shared that whenever she visited her dad's Sierra Leone, *Or Portho*, was what she'd been called - the white girl. Yema's mom was from Russia, where her dad along with most medical doctors in his generation had studied on scholarship. Sharing these names they'd been called in their communities growing up had been an intimate exchange between them. The line they'd crossed to move from being acquaintances to great friends.

"What's up?" Maya asked.

"Been messaging you all day, busy lady. What time should we arrive tonight?" Yema asked.

"Arrive where tonight….oh?" Maya asked

"Oh oh - you forgot?!" Yema countered.

"Oh man!" Maya exclaimed. "I didn't even tell Emmanuel he had to barbecue for us!"

"Well you better get on it! Today is a year since Westgate Mall...we have to be there for Pram." Yema said

"I know, I know - do me a favor then and make yourself useful. Call the others and tell them to come at 6:30pm. That gives me 2 hours to get organized." Maya said.

"Yes ma'am!" Yema answered

Maya had reached her car in the parkade by then. She got in as she hung up, threw her Kate Spade bag in the front passenger seat and sped away.

~~~
~~~

Asma was getting ready to leave the Pharmacy when her phone beeped.

It was a WhatsApp message from Yema to their group - the WOW Pandas.

Gathering is at Maya's as planned - 6:30pm.

Perfect she thought. She was just about done. Asma had chosen to work the 7am - 3pm shift so she could be done on time and finish her paperwork and call-backs before she had to leave. It had worked out perfectly. When her partner at the Pharmacy had suggested that they move to a 24hr service, Asma had resisted the idea, most of all because she didn't want to work shifts. It was very hard for her to adjust in the beginning and she had missed so many WOW Panda get-togethers.

Now that the Pharmacy was running well and they had all the assistants they needed, the system was working for her. She chose shifts that worked around her life. There was always something or the other going on at home with her parents or with one of her 5 brothers and their families. And there was all the babysitting. She loved spending time with her little nieces and nephews. They were her babies for now. She often wondered how all her family obligations would work when she has a family of her own but she chose not to worry about that too much for now. And then, there was The WOW Pandas, *the sisters I never had*, she thought with a smile.

She hung up her lab coat and said her goodbyes. She checked the time - 4:48pm. She headed out to her car, texting Pram as she walked.

Hey - am I still picking you up?

Just done. How about you?

PRAM: Heya. Yep. Almost done here too. Should be ready by the time you get here.

PRAM: May have to wait couple mins when you get here. I'm going over books with Dada now. You know how quickly that goes :)

NOT! :) :) :)...dunno how to do the sticky outty tongue emoticon!

C u soon. Be outside waiting and playing on this thing until you're ready

PRAM: K

PRAM: Thanks love. I need this tonight.

Yeah. We know.

In her car, Asma wondered if she should stop by home to see her parents and freshen up. She decided to. Pram will be a while with her dad anyways. It'll take her 20 minutes to get to the laundromat and she'll likely be waiting just as long, if not longer for Pram to come out. Like Pram, Asma still lived with her parents. Asma lived in an attached suite and Pram had a massive basement suite which was more like a basement palace. It was part of how they connected so well with each other. They understood each other, especially since people here never seemed to understand. "So you still live at home?!" they'd ask. Asma always smiled sweetly and responded unapologetically: "Yes, I do." She'd stopped trying to explain. She was the youngest and only daughter of 6 siblings and her parents were alone now that all her brothers were married and living all over the place. She couldn't imagine leaving her parents entirely by themselves. She'd been raised to understand she had a duty and responsibility to her family and it was just so much a part of her culture. She didn't know otherwise.

She knew that her parents expected her to live with them until she got married, but they didn't take her for granted either. They supported her in working hard and building her business. They were so proud and always bragging about her at their community events.

"This is our baby, Asma, the Pharmacist." She tried not to cringe anymore, accepting that in her community she'll likely always be Asma, the Pharmacist. She much preferred that to being introduced as her parent's daughter or Hamdi's or fill-in-the-blank-with-any-of-her-brothers' sister. She grimaced at the thought that if and when she did get married, she might then be introduced as someone's wife!

Her parents were getting worried. After her 29th birthday this year, Dad kept asking - "Are you sure you don't want us to ask your cousins in Egypt to look around for a match?" "Yes, Dad I'm sure." She'd reply. She was driving now and giggled at her favorite you-need-to-get-married edict of the year. Yesterday, when she again told her dad she was sure she didn't want an arranged marriage in Egypt, her mom had flat-out yelled - "Then arrange it yourself! Get on e-harmony or something." Talk about the tempo rising to desperation! She laughed out loud, thinking about the WOW Pandas faces when she'll tell them tonight. She loved these women. They were her second family. When she goes to Egypt for visits, she loves hanging out with her female cousins since she'd missed out on that growing up abroad. But there was always something missing. That thing is the fact that if she told her cousins about mom's comment they wouldn't find it funny. They would chastise her for laughing about it. The WOWs would laugh along with her.

She messaged Pram again, smiling at the thought of her Indian-Ugandan sista pouring over the books with her dad, trying to slow down for him while glancing frantically out the window to see if Asma had arrived. Time to take some pressure off.

Decided to stop at home. Be there for you at 6, ok. Take your time.

~~~

Ahuva was waiting outside *The Edge Building* for Lina. She leaned against one of the multi-colored twisty posts of the building but it's crisscross lines made it uncomfortable on her back, so instead she
~~~

stepped back to admire it. How did they get each post to be so different, with none of them straight yet still holding up the building? Each post, full of images, recycled materials and random artwork and artifacts. She always found something new every time she examined one of them. This building where she worked was an architectural marvel. She loved it and everything it represented. There were the open office spaces, available for day rentals. There was a gathering spot with *The Edge Cafe* open to the public where only fair trade coffee and organic products were sold. *The Edge Theater*, which did everything from school theatre programs to community productions. The *Edge Art* museum had just opened, showcasing exceptional art from around the world, all created by everyday artists who received a cheque for 70% of all sales of their art. Pieces were flying off the wall since it opened. People loved the eclectic and exotic on this island.

Then there was *The Edge Magazine*, where Ahuva just made Senior Editor. She loved her job. Her magazine, like the building, was an experiment in "learning about sustainability, diversity and equal opportunity at the Edge." The Edge had started as a small non-profit and grew into a huge non-profit society, attracting government funding for all kinds of sustainability and diversity education pilot projects. They were now at the edge of social profit models, researching how to open global stores that will sell international merchandise and accessories produced by everyday local artisans. The idea was that revenues would be split between sustaining the business, paying artisans fairly and then using profits to fund locals to take on projects that will advance development in their communities. Ahuva was staying close to the founders of the Edge and the Board members as the plans unfolded. She intended to be the representative for her native Ethiopia and all of Africa if they went ahead with the plans.

She glanced at her watch. It was 6:05pm and she was starting to get antsy. They'll be late if Lina didn't show-up soon. She heard Lina speeding around the corner before she saw the tiny 2-door Eco-car that they shared screeching toward her. Lina, her crazy roommate was a first-generation Canadian, born to Jamaican immigrant parents.

"Whata gwan gyal!" Lina shouted as she simultaneously leaned over and pushed open the front and only passenger door for Ahuva. When they met as teenagers, Lina used to sound very Canadian, interjecting every second word with "it's like." Sometime around her 21st birthday, she told her friends she'd decided to start going to Jamaica every year and she was going to stop speaking with a perfect Canadian accent when she was around family and friends. "I'll save that for work!" She announced. It was around that same time that she stopped straightening her hair and turned it into locks.

Ahuva laughed as she got into the car. She was tall and lanky and always had to wiggle around to find a comfortable position to fit her legs and the huge hand-woven tote bag she always carried around the bottom of the seat.

"Why don't you just put that damn bag in the back seat!" Lina said.

"Shut-up!" Ahuva replied. She'd learnt to match Lina's tone and general irreverence over the years. "You know I like having it here in case I see something on the way I want to take a pic of or write a note about."

"Ok genius! Can you stop working on this short 15min ride to Maya's place please."

Ahuva ignored her and asked: "How were dance classes today?"

"Oh man!" Lina groaned. "Dem damn adults have 2 lef-feet! I love my kids and teenagers much better, gyal, I'm telling you. Dem young ones may not com into class wit rhythm but they learn movement pretty quick. Once people dem body mature it takes longer to learn movement. Dem white women dema still stressing me wit dem lef-feet and we jus get 2 more classes!"

They were both laughing now but once Ahuva could compose herself, she said: "Hey, some white women do have rhythm." Ahuva had decided she'll never let Lina, any of their friends, or anyone for that matter get away with stereotypical comments. They teased her mercilessly for it but she knew they respected her for it. They called her their conscious.

"Yeah, yeah, yeah! You com and teach wit me all week den tell me dat. When I open my own studio, all of y'all WOW loud mouths ga fi com guest teach different African dances." Lina said.

Ahuva retorted: "Have you seen Yema dance?!"

They howled with laughter.

Ahuva managed a quick: "I rest my case. Some brown and black people can't dance too."

Tears were streaming down Lina's face as she replied: "Yeah - that's a rare ting though and that's coz Yema stayed too long in Russia before she started going back. I told you once dem bones set, you just geh fi learn again. That gyal need fi come to one of my classes!"

~~~

Maya was pleased. The past 2 hours had gone well. She'd called Emmanuel while racing to the grocery store apologizing that she'd forgotten that it was her turn to host the WOWs and would he please please barbecue for them. She admired the table of grilled baby back ribs and burgers now sitting on their dining table. Emmanuel was still out there doing skewered chicken and beef too. She finished putting the paper ware and cutlery out and went outside to give Emmanuel a hug.

"Thanks so much honey...you are too good to me" She said.

Emmanuel pulled her against him with one arm and kissed her forehead while still barbecuing with the other hand. She was petite
~~~

and he was 6ft. She fit perfectly under his arm.

"No wahala. What are husbands for?" He replied. "I'm almost done but I don't expect them to be on time. It's 6:25pm - we probably have at least 15 minutes before the first one arrives.

The bell rang and Maya said: "Oh, you might be wrong!"

"Not a chance," he yelled as she ran inside "It'll be BMT for sure - black man time - that's just the paperboy!"

But instead, he could hear Yema's voice a few minutes later. Then the bell rang again and the door swung open as the ringers let themselves in. It was Ahuva and Lina.

"Hey my African sistas!!"Lina shouted.

They all started laughing, remembering the first time they'd planned a get together and the first time Lina had greeted them with that line. It was early in their first year at Pearson College, the United World College named after Lester B. Pearson, a renowned Canadian Prime Minister and Nobel Peace Prize Laureate. They had seen each other during orientation and Ahuva and Lina found out they were flat mates. They settled into school and were generally friendly with each other. Then, there was a social planned for new students. Maya and Yema hit it off. Across from them on the same table, so did Asma and Pram. Ahuva didn't quite connect with anyone until Asma, who was always outgoing noticed her and invited her to their table. Soon, they were chatting away, laughing, and had a magical evening together. They were amazed at their common connections, at how much they were different, yet the same. They learnt so much about each other and about their various countries and cultures spanning West, East and North Africa, plus Asia and Europe.

At one point that evening, Asma had asked - why doesn't this happen more often? Diverse Africans learning and sharing together. Sharing our unique stories versus the media story of all-Africa.

Imagine that at least 3 of us shared water from the Nile growing up, yet if this were still on the continent, we wouldn't even be connecting or mixing like this. We don't even represent the full diversity of Africa! They should stay close, they agreed. They should keep supporting each other through college and beyond. Yes, Yema had said, that'll be good. Her dad had a group he always got together with in Sierra Leone and they helped each other because as he said, there's a Sierra Leonean parable that: *Rain nor dae fordom na one man dormot - Rain doesn't only fall at one person's door.* They could try something like that. How about a regular meet-up to see how it goes? They planned their first gathering for the next week.

On the day of the first meet-up, Ahuva was getting ready in their flat to leave. Lina looked up from combing her straightened hair and said: "Hey, where are you going?"

Ahuva had hesitated. She wasn't quite sure whether she liked Lina's forwardness in those days.

"Just going to hang out with some of the girls" Ahuva had answered.

"Which girls?" Lina had persisted.

"Oh, just some of the other Africa students" Ahuva had said.

Lina had pouted her lips and shot out: "And who exactly are these African students?!"

"You know, Maya, Yema, Asma and Pram…"

"You mean to tell me you are going to hang out with those multi-colored Africans and leave my black ass here!" Lina had shouted.

"You know," Ahuva said, feeling angry "who told you Africans are only black and who said they are not black!" Ahuva was much more heated about racial profiling and comments in those days.

Lina had stood up, grabbed her jacket and said: "I didn't say they were not black! Well, it's like I'm inviting myself to your little African gathering girlfriend! Coz you know, it's like y'all may be confused, but I am not confused about my African heritage!"

Ahuva had tried to talk her out of it but Lina would have none of it. When they arrived, Ahuva had sheepishly said to the others. "Sorry I didn't tell you I was bringing my roommate Lina…"

"Hey my African sistas!" Lina interrupted. She continued, complete with hip-swaying, finger-wagging sass: "Yeah, it's more like I crashed the party! No way you all are having an AFRICAN party without my proud Jamaican Maroon Akan ass! Heck, you and I could be related Maya! Or even you Yema!

The others stared at her in stunned silence and then burst out laughing. Of course you are welcome to join us! They'd countered. And Ahuva had been embarrassed that she'd tried to dissuade Lina from coming.

They laughed at the memories now as they milled around the table grabbing drinks. "Remember Lina, you're the one who baptized us the WOWs as well!" Yema said.

They'd been at Pram's parents' house at the time. Pram's mom had spoiled them. Filling them up with butter chicken, samosas, rice and lots of snacks. They were complaining about being called minorities, trading stories of being placed in the visible minority box. Ahuva had said matter-of-factly: "What's sad is that we buy into it - so-called minorities are actually the majority number of people in the world you know."

Yema had said: "We should have a code name for ourselves to remind us of that when we're called minorities - like We Are The World. But that doesn't make a good acronym.

Lina had answered: "How bout WOW. We Own the World people! We just WOW!" And the name had stuck.

And then one day, Maya had forwarded a picture to their group on WhatsApp saying: *Should we add Pandas to our name and become the WOW Pandas?* The picture was of a Panda with a caption reading: *Destroy Racism. Be like the Panda! It's black, it's white, it's Asian!* They'd all sent laughing emoticons, and various versions of YES! back.

~~~

They gathered round Emmanuel by the barbecue, thanking him profusely and munching on skewers.

Yema said: "Emmanuel you're a good husband oh! Which African man - Oga man no less - cooks for his wife. And all her friends! Please clone yourself since all your brothers are married oh! We'll even take cousins if they are like you - we'll go visit in Nigeria, just say the word!"

Emmanuel smiled: "Don't mention. It's ok. You ladies are family to us. And yeah, would be nice to have some other brothers join this gathering soon so I can have buddies to have a drink with once y'all are fed and wanna kick me out!"

"I met a white boye I might like" Lina said, sounding oddly embarrassed.

Various versions of oh oh and ah and laughter rose into the air.

"Do tell!!!" Maya squealed.

"Na ah! So I geh fi repeat when Asma and Pram get here! Not happening" Lina said. "Anyone heard from them by the way. It's almost 7pm"

"Well at least someone will be on BMT!" Emmanuel responded.

They all went silent for a minute, the air suddenly solemn with their collective remembering that this was a hard day for Pram. Her sister was an international relations specialist and had moved back to
~~~

Uganda a few years before to work with a Canadian aid agency. While there, she had landed a job with the UNHCR and went often to Kenya's Garissa County to work at the Dadaab refugee camp. She was there in September 2013, and had made a trip into Nairobi to see a good friend who'd just had a baby. Pram and her parents didn't even know that Bindi was in Nairobi when the news of the Westgate Mall terrorist attack hit. They did not find out until afterwards that Bindi and her friend Suki were in the mall with the baby. They were both shot and instantly killed. A kind stranger had grabbed the baby stroller left without an owner and ran to safety with the baby.

The bell rang and all the girls instinctively set down their food and glasses and headed to the door. Asma and Pram walked in and Pram said:

"So sorry we're late! All my fault. We opened late today, coz, you know...the family, we wanted to be together and Dad and I were doing the books tonight so that just took as long as it takes."

Lina said: "gyal, cut de crap and come over here for a hug!"

There in their WOW Pandas circle, Pram at last cried. She'd held it together all day, being strong for her mom and dad. But here, stoic Pram, who always got it done, who always pushed through, could let it go. In their little circle, they had laughed together and cried together so many times.

It was in this same circle, they had cried and waited with Yema for news from home at the height of the war in Sierra Leone. They had come over and stayed up with Maya and Emmanuel when Maya messaged that they were having a hard time. Emmanuel was freaking out because his parents were on a trip to Nigeria to an area where there was a Boko Haram attack. It was the same week Typhoon Koppa hit Philippines and Maya's mom had family in the area most affected. They had watched the news with Asma during the Arab spring, taking turns to help her dial and redial after the phones went down for a while, trying to reach her brother who lived there to make sure he was safe.

And in a few years, they would be distraught when Ahuva will be in the Gaza strip hosting dialogues, a dream she'd always had as a Jewish Ethiopian, when a major attack will happen. They will go to Jamaica with Lina when her brother dies of cancer, and end up welcoming white boye, Peter into their circle with a beautiful impromptu wedding the same week as the funeral. They will discover which one of them will never marry and who will never have children. They will hold each other through births and deaths, moves, divorces and splits in their own circle. But they will fix their splits and grow old doing life together and worrying about what they will do when their own children are as they are now and they have to face the fact that they will have to say goodbye to each other at some point in this life.

In the meantime, they chose to stand in the rain with each other.

9 WHEN I BECAME A BLACK MAN

I could not believe that this was happening to me. I had heard about this. Seen it on the news, but never expected it to happen to me. This, is Canada after all. These things don't happen here. Or so I'd thought.

I felt rage rise up through my chest and explode behind my eyes, filling my vision with white stars. That's why they call it white hot rage, I realized. My heart was pounding in my chest. I heard my mother's voice - my dear crazy mom who explained everything in biological terms saying: *No one can goad you into doing anything wrong when you get angry. Physiologically speaking, the only person who can hijack you is Amygdala. And yours belongs to you! Amygdala will always try to hijack you. But you still have to respond and take action or do something when you are angry. And that, is entirely up to you, mon fils!*

I heard the Black American's voice from the clip my friend Mateo was watching the other day:

Survive the encounter! Don't try to be no hero. Just survive!

I was supposed to be celebrating the start of a dream blossoming. I was feeling like a champion and planning how to break my news to mom and Aunty Moussou tonight when the police cruiser's sirens blinded me. Now, as I watched the cop circle the car and size me up one more time, I realized that today, right now, on this day, a week after my 20th birthday, I have become a black man.

~~~

"AmaduJugor!"

"AmaDU-JUGORRR"

My mom sing-songs my name to get my attention. It was the same thing that morning.

"AmaDU-JUGORRRRRR SOULEYMANE!!!!

When she sings my full name, I know it's time to show-up before she walks in and throws a pillow at me. Or comes into my room, snatches my phone and smacks the back of my head, all while telling me how disrespectful I am and then giving me a list of instructions for the day that I better remember.

I swung my long legs off the bed, turned down the music and went out of my bedroom to meet her.

"Yes, Ma?"

"It's my long day today. I'm at the walk-in clinic this afternoon after my practice, then have hospital rounds tonight. Probably won't be home till midnight."

"Ok. Ma"

"I need you to pick up Aunty Moussoukoro around 9pm for me. She's going to spend the weekend here."

"Sounds good." I smiled, watching her fly around the kitchen, packing her lunch. My mom is a little dynamo. An African Queen. She always wore her hair in tiny braids. She and Aunty Moussou braided each other's hair all the time. She had her braids up in a
~~~

pony. She always did for work to keep it off her face so they didn't interfere with her attending to patients. As always, she looked formal and chic. It's the only way I've seen her look. She was wearing a houndstooth skirt and a frilly yellow-tan silk blouse that was belted. She was wearing the pretty tan wedge-heeled booties I think are cool. She packed her houndstooth purse, checking for her sunglasses. It was one of those lovely spring days out. Still a bit breezy but bright and beautiful with the smell of new blossoms in the air.

"Anything else?" I asked as I helped her into her tan spring jacket.

"Not really...actually yeah - put out the garbage, would you?" She stopped and sized me up. Then grinned and tip-toed to pinch my cheek.

"Mon beau fils!" She exclaimed. "Gloire à Dieu! Just remember who you are AmaduJugor! Be good and remember, you are a child of God, and…"

"You have to first say I am before others will say you are!" We said in unison.

She was laughing as she left, heading to the carport. I watched from the kitchen window as she backed up her black Chevy. I loved how it glimmered in the sunshine, since I was the one who cleaned and waxed it regularly. It looked good on her. I was so proud of her. She waved without fully looking up. She knew I was watching her leave.

~~~

I go by A.J. My mom hates that. It's why she always gives me the 'you have to say I am…" line. She says that's what her dad used to say and that if I don't insist on my identity others will make it up for me. I'm not really fussed about thinking too deeply about those things. A.J. is simple and easy for me and my friends, so A.J. it is.
~~~

My mom's name is Maimounatu Kuyate. Actually, it is Memunatu Kuyate. My mom is originally from Sierra Leone but grew up in Conakry, Guinea, where her family moved during the Sierra Leonean civil war when she was a teenager. That's why she prefers the French-African spelling of her name. It's also why she and Aunty Moussou are inseparable. They grew up in Guinea together, are best friends and nowadays, they just tell people they are sisters. My mom says they may as well be. Look at our names she says. If Aunty Moussou were Sierra Leonean, her name would be Musu Conteh. Across the border, she is Moussoukoro Conte.

I then get the name game from them as they go through Sierra Leonean and Guinean names that are the same.

Diallo and Jalloh

Cisse and Sesay

Camara and Kamara

Sylla and Silla

Not to mention all the others names that are exactly the same for families that live between both countries. Names like Bah, Barrie, Wurie, they'd explain. And then there's all the other Arab names that you might find anywhere in West Africa and elsewhere on the continent from centuries of Arab influence.

Mom says, as for Guinea and Sierra Leone, we are, after all, the same people. She'd say: "Some people just drew a line and said over here, you are British and over here you are French." My mom didn't believe in identifying people by racial labels. I've never heard her say White people. Once when I asked her who she meant by "some people," she smiled and said "Europeans of course - the French, English, Belgians, Spanish, Dutch…I mean the Europeans that settled in Africa before…" I recently realized that I do the same thing. It annoys my friend Mateo. His dad is from Cameroon and his mom is Anglo-Canadian. I swear that kid thinks he's American though. He's always watching YouTube videos and news about the African-American racial situation. His Facebook page is a political statement. He's on a mission to convert me and keeps telling me to "stop being ignorant! These are our issues too." I usually just shrug and change topics. I admire Mateo though. He is knowledgeable, well-spoken and smart. I think he may well be Canada's Obama one day.

After Ma left that morning, I put out the garbage right away so I wouldn't forget. Then, I went back to my room to finish some assignments. I didn't have morning classes. College life was so much better than high school but there was so much more work. I loved the flexibility and independence of it though. I turned my Spotify playlist back on, on my laptop. Drake's *One Dance* was playing. I smiled thinking of Ma and Aunty Moussou. They love this song. It's hilarious watching them dance to it. I had started worrying about how hard it will be on them when I decide to move out. I've been thinking about it but I know mom expects me to stay home through university and save money. Mom will be alone most of the time and that worries me too now that Aunty Moussou had moved so far away because of her work.

I picked up their framed picture from my desk. It was the day of my high-school grad. My mom was as usual formal chic, wearing a pretty floral knee-length dress, with red pumps. She was wearing a knee-length red jacket over it. Aunty Moussou was wearing pants and one of her African print jackets. She was wearing bronze earrings shaped in the African continent - classic Aunty Moussou in her Afrocentric style. Mom is looking up and extending to give Aunty Moussou a high-five with the hand that's free of her clutch. Aunty Moussou is returning the high-five, the edges of her head-scarf blowing in the wind as she leans back in laughter. I can hear her booming laughter through the photo. Her laughter is an unforgettable experience of joy bubbling out of her full-bodied frame like champagne from an uncorked bottle. Aunty Moussou is buxom and I used to love hugs from her as a child. There was something safe and comforting in being cradled with my face buried in the softness of the groove between her breasts. Maybe it was because mom is flat-chested and I didn't get that same comfort cradling from her. They looked so happy in that photo. As they should be. Aunty Moussou has basically raised me with mom. She's like my dad.

I laughed out loud at the memory of the conversation I'd had with them in junior high school. I was so curious about their relationship and how they raised me together. They juggled schedules throughout school to make sure one of them could always watch me. Now that I was a university student, I had come to understand and appreciate more what they had done to care for me with mom in Medical school and Aunty Moussou in graduate school while working a government job. My dad was in town, but mom preferred not to ask him to watch me if she could help it. She'd much rather ask Tante Blessing.

Tante Blessing lived close to the university hospital where mom did her residency and when push came to shove because Aunty Moussou had an exam or something and mom had to be at the university hospital overnight, I had to sleep over at Tante Blessing's place. It was a stuffy two-bedroom basement that always smelled of dried fish and palm oil. Tante Blessing was from The Democratic Republic of Congo but she watched Nigerian movies all day and let me and the other kids stuck at her place eat and do whatever we wanted in the second bedroom. Candy for breakfast was not unusual at Tante Blessing's. She only called one of us kids when she wanted us to pass her something, usually something right next to her like the TV remote. I used to hate being dropped off there, then would love it 2 hours later when I was eating junk and watching shows I wasn't allowed at home, but would be relieved by the time mom or Aunty Moussou showed up for me.

One day, Mom and Aunty Moussou picked me. When we got home, they disappeared into mom's room after dinner as usual. I was a bit older by then and decided to ask them what I had been wondering. I went to the door, hesitated and then barged in.

"Are you two lesbians?!" I asked.

They stared at me. My mom's hands stopped mid-braid in Aunty Moussou's hair and they started laughing. No, they'd said. What made me think that? Maybe because you two always come in here and close the door, I'd explained. That's when Aunty Moussou explained it was because as a Muslim woman who chooses to wear hijab, she didn't want my dad to walk in while she was being braided and see her without her headscarf. Dad still had a house key and tended to walk in unannounced. They went into the room to braid.

Suddenly it all made sense. Aunty Moussou was as devoutly Muslim as mom was devoutly Christian. I'd often wake up to find Aunty Moussou on her prayer mat in the living room early in the morning, while I could hear mom in the spare room saying: "Praise the Lord! Praise Jesus! Hallelujah!" I can tell when mom is worried about something by how fervently and how loudly she prays, switching between French and English. She had been worried that morning. When she came out of her prayer room, I asked her what's up. She'd just smiled and said: "I just felt like spending a bit of extra time praying for you this morning." Me, I'm still non-committal. I grew up in church but mostly just go with mom to make her happy.

~~~

I checked the time. It was 11:30am so I needed to start getting ready. I had two 3-hour classes that day back-to-back at 1pm and 4pm. I also had an 8pm audition so I planned to miss part of my second class to drive the hour and a half across the border to New York for it. I needed to dress so that I could transition for my audition easily. I caught by reflection in the mirror in my room as I stood up. I hated
~~~

that mirror but mom insisted that I have it. "Have you seen any guy with a full-length mirror in their room ever, Ma?!" I'd asked. She'd replied: "Je ne me soucie pas!" *I don't care!* "That's why so many people your age look like hooligans! When you dress, please take a look at yourself and make sure you look decent, ok? S'il tu plaît! No pants on the ground and ball caps in my house!"

The audition instructions said dress smart-casual, prepare to get wet and pack a change of clothes. The instructions also said must be able to swim. I figured that automatically gave me a chance. They were looking for African-Americans and I didn't know many people of African heritage who could swim. I surveyed my closet and decided on a newer pair of jeans and a plain white tee-shirt. I'll wear my Adidas to class with a ball cap. Mom didn't know about the stash of caps at the back of my closet. I decided I'd throw my dark brown belt and matching formal shoes into the car with the fitted navy blazer with denim elbow patches mom bought me to change into for the audition along with my change of clothes. Mom didn't know about the audition either. Every time I thought to tell her that all I wanted to do is act, I can hear her dramatic scream in my mind. She expected me to be academic and go to Med school like her. So far, I was meeting her expectations by being a straight-A science student.

When I decide to tell her, I expect tears and a call to Aunty Moussou. I imagine them giving me the talking to and mom fervently praying the next morning that the devil will lose his grip on me. Then I can't get myself to tell them. Now that I had started auditioning though I needed to tell them sooner than later. I tried on the audition outfit to make sure I liked it. I liked what I saw in the mirror. I'm often called handsome and told I'm a Djimon Hounsou lookalike. I thought people were crazy through my lanky teenage years. After I started playing college football and filled out I could see the resemblance more. I try not to let it get to my head though. The truth is that I'm my father's lookalike.

My dad has now moved back to Bamako, in Mali where he's originally from. We facetime when we can. Dad spent years in France as a teenager and then moved to Montreal in Canada for university. That's where he and mom met. Mom and Aunty Moussou had applied together for post-secondary programs in Brussels, Geneva and Montreal. Montreal won out when mom got into McGill and Aunty Moussou got into the University of Montreal. The beauty and cultural hub of Montreal and its vibrant French-African community had made their transition easy.

Dad was apparently the love of mom's life through university. They stuck together when he dropped out of university to try modelling. Mom still stayed with him when modelling wasn't working out and he started DJ-ing at African clubs. She tried to talk him into going back to school but he wasn't academic like her and he'd called her a snob. But she kept encouraging him. Mom says by the time she got pregnant around the time she was applying for Med Schools, dad was often out drinking with his buddies and stopped coming by. I've heard mom and Aunty Moussou talking about how hard it had been for her to decide to go through with the pregnancy, after dad told her he wasn't interested in being a father yet and that she should consider her options.

The decision was even harder when she got her acceptance into the University of Ottawa's Faculty of Medicine for the next year. Mom had tried again to convince dad. They could move together, she'd persuaded. They could make it in Ottawa if he'd only leave his friends behind and go with her. Dad never showed up at the train station the day Mom left for Ottawa. It was Aunty Moussou who found herself a government job and moved to Ottawa to be with mom and help with me 3 months later.

Dad eventually showed up in Ottawa when I was about 5 years-old. He was broke and trying to get his life back together. There was no love lost between him, mom and Aunty Moussou. He tried to move in with us. Mom told him to get lost. Eventually they agreed he could come visit me and take me out sometimes to get to know me. Mom was done Med-school and was doing her residency by then. A few times, Dad insisted that he could stay with me at our place rather than have me dropped off at Tante Blessing's when mom had a night shift and Aunty Moussou was unavailable. Mom finally acquiesced and gave him a key so he could get in and out and drop me off to school on those mornings when she wasn't back yet.

I noticed that whenever Dad slept over, mom would lock her room door. That was after the time I heard her tell him if he ever tried to go into her room at night again, she'll stab his foot and call the cops on him, telling them he'd attacked her and she'd stabbed him in self-defense. I seriously thought my mom was crazy. I told Aunty Moussou later that Mom had a knife and was planning to kill dad. I couldn't understand at the time why Aunty Moussou laughed herself to tears when I told her what mom had said.

By 12:15pm, I was done. I jumped into mom's old Benz-jeep that she let me use now that I'd gotten my full driver's license. I was a late bloomer with driving. I hadn't taken my Learners' until I was 18. Then with Canada's graduated licensing program, I had to sport an L for Learner until I passed my first driving test, then an N for New driver for 2 years until I passed the re-test. I was so glad to lose that N. I often thought they may as well have us keep the L after passing the initial road test. Because every time someone had sped past me and given me the finger, the N had felt more like L for Loser. I dialed Aunty Moussou on the car-phone planning to lie to her that I'll be late picking her because I have a team meeting with a course group after class. I'll pick her about 10:30pm on my way home from the audition. We'll be home just before mom gets back at midnight.

~~~

I don't remember much about classes that day. My mind was on my audition. I almost chickened out, but then found my nerve again.
~~~

When the lecturer called break during my second class, I asked Mateo if he'd please email me the notes for the second half of class and headed out. The border was only an hour away and the audition location another 30 minutes from there. As I crossed the St Lawrence river, I remembered to take off my ball cap and check for my passport as I rolled into border security. I had crossed this border often with my mom for our New York visits to relatives and her shopping sprees. Still, I was nervous. This was my first trip across alone.

"Hello sir. Passport please," the stern-looking European-American officer said as he eyed me through his glasses.

"Hello sir. Here it is." I replied.

"Please roll down all your windows."

I complied.

"What's your business in the U.S. today?" He asked as he scanned my passport.

"Just going over for an audition meeting" I said, handing him the papers from my agent with the audition details.

He scanned the papers - "you staying overnight?"

"No sir. I'll be back in about two and a half hours, sir"

"What's your occupation?"

"I'm a student at Carleton University, sir."

"So how'd you get this car?"

"It's my mom's car, sir."

"She knows you have it right now?"

"Yes, sir."

My heart was pumping faster now as he walked around, peered into the car and then went back into the booth. He clicked a few times on his system. He seemed to be taking longer than necessary. Finally, he flashed me a smile.

"Good luck on your audition, son!" handing me back my passport.

"Thanks, Sir!" I replied a bit too loudly. I could feel relief and adrenaline surge through me like a current as I speed off. I felt incredibly free.

My nerves and adrenaline levels remained high till I found the location, parked and switched into my belt, shoes and blazer. The throng of young men and women intimidated me. There were at least 100 people there. I felt all energy drain from my body and seep out from under my feet. That was hope leaving me hopeless, I realized. I felt stupid as I stood beside my mom's car, across the border, watching all these fine-looking and swagged-out people competing for the same dream. What the HELL was I thinking! I managed to collect myself and started walking unsteadily forward.

As I approached the venue, I appreciated the medley of beige, brown, bronze and chocolate hues and tones that greeted me. We were grouped by time slots, so I found my group of 10. We awkwardly greeted each other. A hey here, a fist pound there, a brother-man there - then we all hid behind our smart phones. I started pulling out my phone and then decided not to. Instead, I leaned comfortably against a wall with my hands in my pocket and watched as people took selfies and posted endlessly on social media. I tried not to check the time every minute. The 15 minutes I had to wait felt like hours and I felt stupider every second. The guy next to me didn't look like he was going to make it. He kept going into the Porta Potty. He looked like he'd throw up any minute. I subtly moved further down the wall away from him. His nerves were escalating mine and I didn't need his puke on me if it happened.

Suddenly the door opened and I heard a voice say:

"Group K please! That'll be Mark, Dashon, Ryker, A.J…."

I didn't hear or remember anything clearly after I heard A.J. I remember thinking - *Group K! that's 10 groups they've seen already! What the HELL am I thinking!* I also remember whispering a prayer. *Jesus help me!* I remember bright lights. Then I remember being handed a script with 15 minutes to prepare. The next thing I'm standing in front of the crew and I hear: TAKE 1 of 1! ACTION! \Ten minutes later I was embracing the European-American girl I'd just saved after tossing my wine glass, throwing off my jacket and shoes and jumping into the pool in the middle of the auditorium. I'm staring into the eyes of forbidden love and passion rising between us. AND CUT!

~~~

They asked me to stay and do another take. I was confused. Wasn't there only one take for each person's audition. Yes, but they wanted to see me again. I was the first *interesting* audition they'd seen all evening. And they had auditioned for this role across 3 cities already. By the time I'd changed from my wet clothes and left the auditorium heading back to my mom's car in the parking lot, I was inflated with hope again. I knew they had at least another 90 people to see. The last group in line was Group T. But I was *interesting*! I needed to tell mom and Aunty Moussou tonight. They said they expected to call my agent tomorrow. What if I got it?! What if I got it?!

I don't remember getting back to the border, but soon I was throwing off my ball cap and passing my passport back to the Canada Border Services Agency Officer who greeted me with:

"Good Evening. Bonsoir."

"How long have you been gone?"
~~~

"Where have you been tonight?"

"Did you buy anything across the border?"

"Bringing any alcohol or substances back, sir"

He signaled his colleague who was walking dogs around cars to walk around mine. The dog didn't start barking furiously after walking around the car so the officer said:

"Welcome home - have a good night!"

I drove off, my mind still racing. It was 15 minutes before I remembered I had to head to Aunty Moussou's first and I didn't know the way from the border. Her new address was saved on my phone which was signaling low battery. I pulled off the highway. There was a parallel dirt road beside the highway that led to a small unmarked parking lot. It looked like a rest stop. It was poorly lit but was close to the freeway and there was a lit-up strip mall across the street so I pulled in. There was one car across from me and I saw some teens get out and lean against the car smoking. I rolled up my open front windows and hit the automatic lock on the car door, then plugged in my phone, looking up the address and putting it into the GPS.

Mom and Aunty Moussou, I need to talk to you…

No that'll sound too ominous.

Hey, I have some good news for you...

No, too fake.

Maybe straight up...I want to be an actor. I auditioned today and it's possible I'll be offered a part tomorrow. Will you support me to do it if I got it?

I heard my mom screaming in my mind.

I saw a car roll by out of the corner of my left eye.

Maybe I should tell Aunty Moussou first when I pick her up. She could advise me on how to tell Mom. She's a bit less dramatic and more reasonable sometimes.

Aunty Moussou….

The bright lights blinded me. The car that rolled by was an unmarked police car. The next thing I know I am standing beside my car with my hands behind my head.

Survive the encounter!

Now, I see my mom leaving home this morning and waving to me. I see myself heading off to class. I recall the medley of people who look like me that I just left behind in New York State. I wonder if they all made it home safe or if any of them are having this experience that I am now having. I bite my lip to keep from screaming as the cop frisks me, hitting my legs wider with his baton.

Survive the encounter!

I remember my mom and Aunty Moussou talking with alarm about the rising number of shootings of unarmed African-Americans during the protests following the Akai Gurley shootings in New York. This is not new they said. And we immigrant Africans are not exempt! Remember Amadou Diallo. Aunty Moussou's family actually knew some of Amadou's relatives back in Conakry when it had happened.

Tears of rage and frustration roll down my face. The cop leaves me standing in the cold for what seems like an eternity. He finally returns and tells me I can go.

My hands are shaking on the steering wheel when I get into it to drive. I don't know how I make it to Aunty Moussou's but I do. I also don't know how I manage to fake it till we get home.

~~~
~~~

At home, I plead exhaustion and excuse myself to my room. I google black profiling and policing in Canada. I surf and read about the profiling issues in Ontario. I find Desmond Cole's article - *This Skin I'm in* - about being carded 50+ times in the Toronto area. I feel a kinship with Desmond because he has Sierra Leonean heritage. I am both comforted and troubled by the chronicles of his experience.

I pick up my phone and start a Facebook post. I don't know that it'll help but I guess this is how my generation shares our woes and tells our stories. I write in my status:

> What's on my mind?! Today, I pulled off the highway into a parking lot to charge my phone and plug in the address to pick-up Aunty @Moussoukoro. There were three kids smoking weed nearby in the only other car in the lot. So I rolled up my window to keep the smell out my car. A cop rolled by, clearly smelling it because his windows were down. He pulls into the lot, parks across from me and blinds his lights right at me through the windshield. These kids put out the joint and "act natural." The cop gets outs and taps my window. I roll down my window:
>
> Cop: Hello how are you today?
>
> Me: I'm good sir. And yourself?
>
> Cop: Good. So do you know why I'm smelling Marijuana in the area?
>
> Me: I believe the kids over there were smoking
>
> Cop: ok, can you step out of your car sir? Hands on your head please and lean against the car!
>
> After getting close to smell my breath, checking the interior of my car, asking me a bunch of questions, frisking me and realizing I had no illegal substances on me, he leaves me in

the cold for a while. I think he was in his car pulling up my license and checking my mom @Maimounatu's car plates. I was too freaked out to turn and look in case he freaks and shoots me. He eventually walks back to me and says "Looks all good. Have a nice day."

Now I watch the cop to see if he would talk to these 3 white kids about it. Instead, he hops in his car, and drives off as if to say he did his job. Now I try to understand situations to prevent myself from screaming racism every chance I get. But I cannot see any other possibility. I was profiled as a dealer or smoker because of my age, gender, race and the car I was driving. I can no longer deny that in others' eyes, I am first and foremost a black man. Today, I was initiated. It's sad to know that even in a country where I may not become a hashtag because of gun violence, I am still profiled.

Racism is alive and well people. All l can do is pray for the people with this mentality to stop seeing stereotypes and pray for future generations to be better than ours. I can't do anything about the cop's blatant racism. But I won't let his ignorance affect my future and I can't be ignorant anymore. One wrong action or word and I'm in cuffs.

If you are racially profiled like I was today, don't allow them to win. Don't be the stereotype they want you to be. Continue to be the best version of you. And by the way, for those of you who know me as A.J., my full name is AmaduJugor Souleymane. It's sounds exactly as it is spelt: A-ma-du-Jug-or Sou-ley-ma-ne. Please learn to say my name. I will still answer to A.J., but I'll remind and ask you to call me AmaduJugor from now on. Peace! Matthew 5:44[3]

---

[3] Tribute to my nephew Adeyemi Taylor-Lewis aka Dey who let me use and adapt his real Facebook post for this story. Dey is a college student and singer songwriter who was born and lives in Vancouver, British Columbia.

I put my phone down and go to bed. Mom and Aunty Moussou will see my post and we will have lots to talk about in the morning. I think I'll call Mateo tomorrow too...

10 THE WEDDING

♪ ♪ *We Yawoo fine oh!* ♪ ♪

♪ ♪ *We Yawoo fine oh!* ♪ ♪

♪ ♪ *How we manage so tay we yawoo fine so!* ♪ ♪

♪ ♪ *Ar say, we yawoo fine oh! We yawoo fine so!* ♪ ♪

♪ ♪ *How we manage so tay we yawoo fine so!* ♪ ♪

Our bride is beautiful, our bride is beautiful, how did we get a bride so beautiful!

The goombay drummer pounded away at the drum, his hands and head flying in unison as he rocked to his goombay beat. All around him were swirls of bright colors and West African print as people rolled up and down and around. Hips, hands and feet in rhythm to the music. It was a Sierra Leonean wedding and Shawn could not believe he was at the center of it all.

♪ ♪ *All dem bella dem sidom na we dey go so mama ya!* ♪ ♪

♪ ♪ *All dem bella dem sidom na we dey go so mama ya!* ♪ ♪

Shawn watched his beaming bride.

"What are they singing now?!" He shouted above the music.

She laughed that hearty laugh of hers: "Something along the lines of all the onlookers are watching and away we go...as in, boo to all the haters!"

He laughed and drew her close.

God, she was beautiful, smart and sexy, he thought. It was a beautiful sunny day in Freetown, Sierra Leone; with the rainy season just a couple of months past, the flowers and vegetation were in full bloom and everyone was dressed in their finest. The service had been absolutely great and held in a quaint colonial church halfway up the mountains overlooking the western part of Freetown. He could hardly believe that this day had happened, was happening. He had always wondered about Africa, wondered if he'd ever make the journey. It was everything he expected and nothing like he'd imagined. And to come here this way was much more than icing on the cake. He was in awe of the paths and journeys of life that weave and blend people together. Of the road that always leads exactly to where you ought to be. He was in awe of God. He couldn't wait to share stories and pictures when they got back to their other home to visit - Nova Scotia, Canada.

~~~

Shawn Clarkson was intrigued by the girl in cornrows. She looked foreign and yet not. He had an eerie sense of familiarity toward her. The kind of déjà vu feeling you get when you meet someone you think you've met before but know you haven't. She also looked comfortable and yet not. She wore an air of confidence about her like a familiar sweater. Yet it was clear she was out of place. For one thing, it was early fall in Ottawa, Canada, and she was wearing red high-heels and the blouse and leather jacket she had on didn't look warm enough. She also alternated between gazing out the window and checking some information in the papers in her hand and on her phone.
~~~

She looked new to town, but didn't have the confused anxious look of someone who didn't know where they were going or what they were doing. He'd caught her eye briefly above the commuter paper he was reading. He'd smiled and she'd flashed him a smile back that surprised him. It was a genuine, full smile that curled her full upper lip and made her eyes glimmer. It wasn't the standard Canadian smile - that flash of teeth that stranger's shared here, which was an automatic and mere acknowledgment of others. It was probably the smile he had given her, because he could do it in his sleep. *I don't want her to ever lose that smile* he found himself thinking, surprising himself again. That's when he decided to go over to her. He took the bus to avoid rush hour traffic and only used his car on evenings and weekends. He'd never approached a girl on the bus before.

He walked across the bus towards her. She lifted her head and flashed that smile again, holding his eyes and then examining his face. Her face was interesting. She had deep, thoughtful eyes, like there was a lot going on behind them all the time. They drew him in like her smile had, because he didn't know anyone who's eyes conveyed deep interest toward a stranger like hers did. They were narrow and small, almost Asian-looking eyes that looked out of place in her dark chocolate face. Her nose was small and cheekbones square, making her face striking. Her lips were very full, proportionally bigger than the rest of her face. He got to her and said simply:

"Hi. My name is Shawn Clarkson. What's yours?"

"Baindu. Baindu Koroma." She replied.

Her voice was deep and melodic. She had an accent that Shawn could not place.

"I hear an accent - where are you from?" Shawn asked.

Baindu's eyes flashed. He could sense her annoyance and irritation.

"Well, it's a long story…how about you tell me where you're from first" she stated emphatically, sizing him up.

"Ok, I'm from Jordantown, Nova Scotia." He replied "I have a long story too. Now what's your long story."

She looked obstinate for a second. Perhaps she sensed his determination to stay put and keep talking to her, so she explained.

"I think of myself as African, but if I say only that, I leave the 'Africa is a country' image with you. I wish I didn't have to start every conversation explaining myself. I'm from a tiny country on the West Coast of Africa called Sierra Leone. But I was born in Geneva, went back to Sierra Leone when I was 5 for 5 years, then lived and travelled to Congo, Sudan, Rwanda, Ethiopia and Angola an average of 3 years each before moving here for grad school. We also travelled quite a bit in and out of Southern Africa to Botswana, South Africa and Mozambique for visits as well as a few other West African countries too – Ghana, Nigerian, Ivory Coast, Liberia, Benin…"

Shawn's eyebrows were raised by now.

"Yeah, see what I mean?!" Baindu said

"Yes, I see. I want to say sorry I asked but I'm not really sorry" For some reason he found himself giving her his hand to shake and grinning. "Pleasure to meet you. You're the first Sierra Leonean I've met – it's ok to say you're Sierra Leonean, right?"

"Yep! My parents are back there now."

"Then that could be your short answer, like Nova Scotia is my short answer." He said.

"Somehow I didn't think that'll satisfy you" She answered.

He looked at her, perplexed that she didn't seem curious about his being from Nova Scotia. He opened his mouth to ask her about it and said instead:

"So you're here for grad school?"

"Yes," she answered. 'University of Ottawa, Masters in Education."

"Again, pleasure to meet you! I'm the Dean of Faculty Development and Research for the Social Sciences department there."

"Oh," she said sounding unimpressed. "what does a Dean of Faculty Development and Research do since it's not a discipline of study?"

"I basically help faculty members find research funding and opportunities, do and share their research with other faculty and look for opportunities to collaborate."

"Oh!" she said again. "Do you also teach?"

"Yes, my focus is in International Development and Global Studies although I don't teach a full course load because of all my other administrative responsibilities."

"Oh ok." She looked accepting but unsure. "Here's my card he offered, fishing one out of his laptop bag. If you ever need help getting around campus, call me. My cell's on there as well."

She hesitated for a second and then took the card. "Thank you" she muttered.

Shawn decided to ask: "Forgive my curiosity but I'm going to pry some more. Why were you born in Geneva and why did you travel so much? What did your parents do?"

"My dad was a diplomat and my mom worked for UN and a few other international agencies."

"Oh," it was Shawn's turn to say, "so you're an African elite. Makes sense now." He sounded edgier than he'd meant to, his tone laced with the aftertaste of his years of studying Africa's colonial and post-colonial history. He was well aware of the current wealth inequalities perpetuated by corrupt leaders and in his mind, condoned by the elite whose lifestyles blinded them to the plight of the less educated and disadvantaged majority.

"Well, um, I guess you could say that." She replied, looking conflicted too.

There was an uncomfortable silence between them. Shawn felt the tension of his thoughts battling with his desire to know her more. He'd enjoyed her directness too. She hadn't balked or deferred to his status as a faculty administrator as often happens with students.

"Well here we are." She said as they pulled into the university bus loop. She stood up, preparing to leave and signaling the conversation was over.

"See you around?" Shawn ventured.

"Yes, see you around," she replied, getting off the bus and walking away rapidly in the opposite direction.

He noticed he was worried about how long she'd last in that jacket and those shoes. He also noticed that she was curvy and shapely. Like her lips, her behind seemed proportionally larger than the rest of her body, yet suited her perfectly.

~~~

Baindu found the Faculty of Education and did all her registration and paperwork that day. She found herself thinking about Shawn Clarkson whenever she had a minute. It was a strange encounter she thought. She wasn't sure if she liked him. He had the air of those that thought they knew too much already. His African elite comment had stung and gnawed at her. Who was he to judge? He didn't even know
~~~

her.

He was average height for a guy – probably 5ft 10 inches over her 5ft 6inches. He was a bit on the skinny side for her liking though. She reckoned he was at least 10 years older than her. She did like his style. His khaki pants went well with the beige checkered beret he'd been wearing. His blue and brown pinstriped shirt blended perfectly with his brown jacket too. He looked smart she thought. She noticed he'd been looking at her shoes and jacket which embarrassed her. She'd almost slipped on her heels a few times already. The floors were getting slippery as it got colder outside. She hadn't brought any fall or winter clothes with her. She decided she would get off the bus at the mall on the way home and buy boots and 5 turtleneck sweaters in different colors.

When Baindu got home from Sears with her shopping bags, Uncle Fofana was having dinner. It was rice and cassava leaves.

"Good evening Uncle" she offered.

"Ah, good evening Baindu. How was your day at University? Did you get most things done?" She noticed he loved using the words more and most incorrectly. She suppressed the urge to ask him whether he meant to ask if she'd finished everything on her list.

"Yes, Uncle," she responded. He was chewing very loudly and Baindu tried to hide the look of disdain she could feel growing on her face. She had been surprised several times over the 2 weeks she'd been staying with them at his crass manners.

"I see you went shopping." He observed eyeing her bags and then eyeing her.

She felt mildly uncomfortable under his gaze as she said: "yes, I needed some warm clothes. I felt cold today."

"Where's Aunty Mabinty?" she asked.

"Oh she's out. Make yourself comfortable" he said while chewing through the food in his mouth. "Put your stuff down and join me for dinner. Aunty also left some okra and foofoo too so you can have either that or the rice and cassava leaves. She had also made ginger beer"

Baindu nodded in agreement and headed to the room where she was staying with her bags. It was Uncle Fofana's daughter's room before she went to college and it still looked like a teenager's room. There was a "KNOCK BEFORE YOU ENTER AND DO NOT ENTER UNLESS I SAY SO" sign on the door. Girlfriend even locked her parents out during the day. Aunty Mabinty had sheepishly handed Baindu a key when she arrived saying:

"Here's the key...you know how children here are nowadays with all their rights. Hawa wanted her privacy so she put a lock."

Baindu wondered what the girl with a sign like that, a door lock and *I love punk and rock* posters in her room was like. She could not understand how a Sierra Leonean family would tolerate that behavior. She imagined her mom tearing the sign off the door in full-on crazy African mother drama. Her mom would ask her what kind of crazy she'd become and tell her that she could have a sign like that after she started paying bills in her own house! She smiled as she thought that she wouldn't put it past her mom to unhinge the door completely if she had ever dared putting up a sign like that.

No matter where they went in the world, her parents had instilled a strong sense of respect for elders and the importance of participating in family and community rituals in her. Her parents were worldly-wise yet traditional at the same time. Her mom would say, "You are Sierra Leonean and African first before anything else, so I expect you to behave that way!" It was the only reason she was going to join Uncle Fofana for dinner. She did not want to appear rude. It was also the reason she called them Aunty and Uncle - they weren't really relatives. They were not even the kind of honorary uncles and aunties she'd grown up knowing. They knew no one else in Ottawa and a friend of her parents had made the connection and introduction. Her parents had accepted their offer to host her until she found her feet. They felt better they'd told her, that she would stay with someone from the community until she settled.

Baindu could sense she wasn't going to last there. Uncle Fofana generally tried too hard and she couldn't stand the way he treated Aunty Mabinty while she waited on him hand and foot.

Baindu quickly changed and joined Uncle Fofana. She settled on a very small bowl of rice and okra and poured herself a big glass of chilled ginger beer.

"You won't have foofoo with your okra?!" Uncle Fofana asked incredulously

She loved okra, but found the mound of pounded, fermented and cooked cassava called foofoo too starchy and bland for her liking. She never really liked it growing up.

"I prefer rice with it, thank you" Baindu replied.

"But it is more better with foofoo!" He replied.

Baindu suppressed a sigh. She turned around to head to the table and felt another wave of discomfort at the way Uncle Fofana was staring at her underneath his eyelids, a handful of foofoo poised for his mouth. His cleaned plate of cassava leaves was pushed away from him as he worked on his foofoo bowl for his second serving. He lowered his gaze when he saw her watching him and stuck his fingers back into the bowl. She wondered how she was going to make it through dinner.

As she sat down, they heard the front door opening and Aunty Mabinty walked in, with shopping bags, wiping her feet on the welcome mat.

"Good evening, good evening, kushe oh! Sorry I'm late for dinner, the bus was late today."

Uncle Fofana grunted a response and looked instantly annoyed. Baindu got up to help Aunty Mabinty with the bags, breathing a sigh of relief and feeling angry that Aunty did the groceries on the bus at the end of her day, while Uncle Fofana came home with the car to eat the food she'd woken up early to cook before going to work. Uncle Fofana also did not offer to help with the bags. Baindu didn't understand how Aunty Mabinty managed to stay so pleasant and why she said nothing. By the time they were finished moving the bags of groceries to the kitchen, Uncle Fofana had disappeared into the living room and the sound of Anderson Cooper on CNN was floating their way. His dirty dishes were still on the table.

~~~

Shawn couldn't stop thinking about the girl with the cornrows. He found himself practicing her name the way he'd heard her say it, repeating it over and over again. Ba-in-du. No, Bai-ndu. That wasn't quite right either. Bain-du. He loved the sound of it. He had looked her up in the student information system. He felt guilty doing it but now he knew the spelling of her name which had helped him with his obsessive practicing of it. He also now knew she was very smart. She'd gotten into grad school as a straight-A undergraduate student. He kept looking for her on the bus every week after he'd seen her but never saw her again.

A month later, he had stopped looking for her on the bus but started making excuses to go by the Education Faculty. He decided he'll call his friend Richard tomorrow. Richard was his running buddy and a new professor in the Education faculty. Shawn had been holding out because he didn't want to acknowledge he was obsessed after a chance encounter or deal with too many questions or cautions from Richard. He knew full well he knew nothing about the girl outside of their conversation and his breach of student privacy.
~~~

His cell phone rang and he picked it up absentmindedly. He was in the kitchen of his condo, chopping veggies to make a stir fry for dinner.

"Hello. I know you don't know me and this may be inappropriate but I need help."

Baindu's unmistakable accent and clear bold tone caught him off guard. He felt a pinch in his hand and realized he had nicked his finger.

"Oh hey, hello Bain-du. What's wrong?" He managed, suddenly feeling the same rush of protectiveness he'd felt watching her walk away from the bus the month before. "Are you okay?"

"No, I'm not okay. I'm at the library on campus, can you meet me...please." He heard her say.

"I'm not on campus, but...stay put. Wait for me in the front reading area." Shawn grabbed his hat and the keys from the hook by his front door. Five minutes later he had taken the elevator to his basement parkade, jumped in his car and was speeding off to the campus library.

When Shawn got there, Baindu looked like she'd been crying. Her eyes were red and she had a carryall suitcase with her.

Shawn approached her and said nothing, just eyeing her and the suitcase with a raised brow.

"I would go to a hotel/motel but I don't want to be alone right now and I can't use my student allowance on a hotel bill. I've been wading off advances from my non-uncle uncle where I've been staying but he's been getting more aggressive. I got a place but need to wait a week to get in so I thought I'd just ride it out and I've been locking my door. I came from the bathroom this evening though and found him in my room, in his daughter's old bed, clothes on the floor. Said

I need to stop pretending I don't know he wants to take care of me. He threatened to tell my parents I'd been soliciting him if I said no. Luckily, I had their punk-ass daughter's wrist key ring coz I wanted to use the mini scissors on it to open some new cosmetics in the bathroom. I walked out and locked him in the room. I waited in my towel sitting outside the door and listening to him hurling insults and threats at me till Aunty got home an hour later."

Shawn felt hot with anger, but managed to ask: "what happened then?"

"I told her obviously. We opened the door and he tried to say it was me and I had locked him up coz he refused me. I left her beating him with a pillow and whatever she could lay her hands on while I threw on clothes and the stuff in the bag. He threatened to beat her up if she didn't stop and I told him I was already going to file a statement with the police and would call 911 right there if he hit her."

She pulled her sweater tighter and Shawn said: "Give me your bag. I'll take you to my place. I was cooking dinner. You can eat and we'll go from there."

She hesitated, then looked at him with flashing eyes.

"I didn't have anyone else to call but you seemed kind and authentic the other day. I figured you're another man, but you are also a university professor and administrator in Canada and wouldn't do anything stupid. Plus, I did file that police report and I told them I'll call back with the address where I'm going. So, if you agree to give me your address and let me give it to them with your number and promise not to even dream of taking advantage of me, I'll come with you."

He smiled a somber smile. He loved her wisdom, clarity and boldness. "You've got it. My address is…"

~~~
~~~

Baindu stayed at his place for the week. He gave her his bedroom which had a lock and he slept on the couch. They commuted to campus together and he noticed how visibly relaxed she became whenever they left the apartment and were in the open air. It saddened and angered him. He also noticed that she tried to rearrange her study groups to make sure she could bus home with him when he finished work at 5pm. It was fully fall by then and getting dark by 4pm. He realized she didn't want to be alone on transit in the dark.

Once home though, she was cagey and withdrawn, often claiming to be tired and going to the room at her first opportunity. The door always clicked behind her. He stayed out of her way and didn’t ask her for any more details unless she offered. He only interfered when he heard her arguing with her parents about the police report and follow-up. She'd gotten loud on the phone, sounding angry and frustrated. He deciphered they wanted her to drop the charges. That day, after she hung up he knocked gently on the door. When she opened it a crack, he said simply:

“I'll drive you down to the station to complete the report if you like. I think you should file it. Don't let the bastard get off free.”

She'd silently grabbed her bag and let him drive her to the station.

At the end of the week he was sad to see her go. Her new place was right by the campus though, so he knew she'd be safe. Over the next few months he checked on her regularly and he invited her for dinner at least once a week. She always hesitated but always came unless she was studying for an exam. The day she agreed to come even though she had an exam the next day, Shawn felt like the sky had opened. She studied at the dining table and he served her dinner and washed up while he watched her and enjoyed her presence in his space. That was the first day after her week of refuge that she slept over again. Shawn didn't sleep well on the couch that night. He lay there flipping channels, wondering whether she slept on her back or side and what it would be like to listen to her breathing in her sleep.

The next week, she offered to come herself. After dinner, they washed up the dishes together. As they finished, Shawn turned to face her. He put his wet hands gently on her shoulders and opened his mouth, not sure what he wanted to say. She simply put a finger on his lips, said "shhhh" and kissed him. That day, the sky parted and he heard angels singing. They sat together on the couch watching sports and news all evening. She fell asleep on the couch, her head resting against his shoulder. He laid her head down on his lap and covered her. He listened to her breathing until he fell asleep too.

In the morning, she was up before him. When he woke up, he was lying fully on the couch and covered and she was staring at him. She said:

"I'll come as often as you want but I'll keep my place. My parents will flip out if they find out I gave up my place and live with some guy. I'm also not ready to go to bed with you...yet. This might sound strange to you but I've never been with a man and I'd like to keep it that way. I dream of saving myself for my wedding day but I'm not asking you to be my husband either so don't panic!"

Shawn couldn't wipe the silly grin off his face.

~~~

They courted for a year. Shawn's running buddy Richard, kept telling him he was crazy. "You should end this madness," Richard said. "What kind of 25-year old isn't sexually active. It's too good to be true, man, she's playing you."

Other times he'd be like "Man you sound like a married man who isn't getting game with his own wife! You even go to church with her!"
~~~

Shawn finally asked Richard to cut it out the day he said "you sure she isn't stringing you along coz she wants you to marry her...you know...being African and all. You sure it isn't about the papers."

About a year after their 1st anniversary, Shawn told Baindu they were going on a weekend trip for Thanksgiving. He picked her up from her place and drove straight to the airport. They flew to Nova Scotia. They spent a night in Halifax the first day, because Shawn wanted to show her the city. Then there was a surprise he said, before they went into Jordantown for a day so she could see where he was from and meet his family.

The next day after breakfast, Shawn finally told her the surprise. He was taking her to see the new Black Loyalist Heritage Centre in Shelburne.

"I decided I wanted to do this from the day I met you. I was annoyed that day on the bus because I couldn't believe the fact that I'm black from Nova Scotia and you're from Sierra Leone didn't spark any connection for you. My friend Patrick Foon from Liberia was the same way when we were in college and he used to shrug whenever I tried to get into it. I mean, what history do they teach you bourgeoisie Africans over there anyway."

Baindu replied matter-of-factly: "European history! Colonialism may be officially done but we're still a colonized people on the continent remember!"

"Well…not only on the continent babe. Here too. And part of being free is knowing our heritage. Let's go."

Five hours later, they were standing at the big beautiful glass windows overlooking Birchtown Bay and the breathtaking Shelburne Harbour and Baindu was still vibrating.

"Oh my God, thank you so much for bringing me here. I'm going to go through your bookshelves and read-up. OMG!" she said again, wiping a tear from her cheek.

She'd learned the story of how the Black loyalists came to Nova Scotia for the promise of freedom after the American Revolution, only to be met with impossible conditions and hardships. She had wept when they viewed the replica of the pit houses that Blacks built and lived in to survive the harsh winter, as they awaited land grants from the government.

They'd gone to the Old School House and the Saint Paul's Church. When they viewed the Bunce Island exhibit and movie, Baindu kept exclaiming "I've been there on one of our Christmas visits home to Sierra Leone!!"

Going through the virtual Carlton's Book of Negroes was an experience she will never forget. There were so many last names of Freetown Creole families she knew. She kept wondering which of the names she recognized were the direct descendants of the people in this book.

She squealed when she saw Thomas Peters' name and read about his fight for land rights for the Black settlers and the plan for the journey back to Africa to start the new settlement in Freetown in 1792.

Shawn had shared his own long identity story. "My several-times great granddad was apparently one of the ones who decided to stay behind to mind the settlers who were staying and keep trying to improve conditions. Here is his name in the Book - Eric Johnson. The story is that he changed his name from Eric Johnson to Eric Thomas-Clarkson. Said if he was going to have a white man's name then he'd rather have the name of one that helped his people get to freedom than one that enslaved him. We have records showing his signature as Eric Johnson and then showing the switch. I dropped the Thomas part of the last name as soon as I could, just so I wouldn't have a hyphenated name anymore. Most of the family still uses the full Thomas-Clarkson last name."

Baindu could only manage a "wow!"

Suddenly Shawn said sheepishly: "what if we are related? We wouldn't know."

She looked at him, head tilted, and said: "Not likely. You'd need to do the DNA test and tracing to know if Sierra Leone is where you were originally from. Like the South Carolina Gullahs and Geechees. Your lineage could be from anywhere where slaves were originally taken. And if at all you are from Sierra Leone, I'm Mende, the majority ethnic group and as far as we know not of slave descent. I have no way of knowing if my ancestors were part of the trade. I equally have no way of knowing if parts of our family were taken, but if they were and you are a descendent from a Mende relative of mine, we are far enough removed by now that it wouldn't matter."

"Then Baindu Koroma, I'd like to ask you to marry me." Shawn said simply.

Baindu felt light and breathless. This was too much for one day. Shawn pulled out the simple box from his pocket. Baindu gasped through tears as he opened the box to reveal a simple ring set with a peridot stone for her birth month, August. They had discussed the complexities of Blood Diamonds one evening and Baindu had insisted that given the connection between blood diamonds and Sierra Leone she didn't even want so-called clean/certified diamonds when she got married. She wanted a simple ring with her birthstone or any other gem, just not diamonds. Baindu looked at Shawn and asked: "Are you sure?" He said yes and she said yes. Shawn felt goosebumps rise through his back and neck in that moment. He thought he heard his ancestors applauding as they watched the sunset through the glass windows.

They walked the Heritage Trail afterwards, feeling a profound sense of rightness as they walked where those before them had, embracing and silently savoring the moment. They left a virtual quilt on their way out that read: *Shawn and Baindu said Yes! here: To freedom, love and our heritage and roots!*

~~~

The next day, they got up early and drove to Jordantown. It was Sunday and their arrival brought much yelling of Hallelujahs as the family walked together to church. Baindu was overwhelmed with a sense of familiarity and kept telling Shawn how the elderly women and the women in his family in their church hats and beads looked exactly like the Creole women who attended the Trinity or Cathedral or Saint John churches in Freetown. They traded off educating each other as Baindu now explained the explosion of missionary work in Sierra Leone after the colony was established. That she knew, she said, because she went to a Methodist elementary school because it was the best in town at the time. She'd learnt about the history of the schools and churches in Sierra Leone then, but none of this heritage stuff.

Their time at Jordantown went by too quickly. His family blessed them and sent them on their way. Shawn had lost both parents so his aunt who raised him and a couple of other relatives said they would get on with getting their passports if the wedding was going to be in Freetown. They would not send him off like an orphan, no sirree. And imagine, they said, making the journey Eric Thomas-Clarkson had never made!

Back in Ottawa, they set out to start planning. Baindu called home. Her parents were thrilled at the news. They would welcome Shawn they said, but he must do everything right! They must marry in Freetown and there would be a traditional wedding and a church wedding. Baindu advised Shawn to say yes to everything. So he did. She told him to call everyone Aunty and Uncle, so he did that too. The date was set for the week before Christmas. It was a struggle to get a date, his mother told him. The Anglican church didn't like marrying people during Christmas but they said they'd make an
~~~

exception only because they were coming from abroad, given the circumstances.

Baindu warned Shawn to brace himself for the Freetown experience. She tried to explain all the things she thought would be a culture-shock and then gave up and decided to let him have his experience. Shawn had barely spoken between their landing at Lungi airport and their journey to Baindu's parent's home at Spur loop Freetown. He looked dazed at the airport, watching the chaos and commotion but they somehow made it through with all their suitcases. He'd watched Baindu haggle with immigration officers in Krio and Mende when they tried to overcharge them for their landing visas. Then he'd been amazed when a porter went from being aggressive to deferent when he realized who Baindu's family was.

He shouted: whooo! at the onslaught of porters and pan-handlers that greeted them on the way to the car waiting for them. Then was taken aback by the driver standing by the Mercedes who greeted them as "Mr. Clarkson, Sir" and "Hello Ms. Baindu." They had to take the ferry he said, helicopter and float plane services were down. Her parents were waiting to receive them at home. Baindu groaned, warning Shawn to brace for the ferry ride. Nothing could have prepared him for the cacophony of sight, sounds and the sheer volume of people on the ferry. They had to push their way through the throngs of people and through the smells of fish, sweat and seawater intermingled with the smell of urine that greeted them yards away from the public-use toilets.

Two minutes later he was shocked when they entered the VIP lounge with a bar, a clean toilet and stations where passengers in suits worked and chatted while their laptops and mobiles charged. He sighed with relief, the familiarity of the space enveloping him like the warmth of the Freetown sunlight. Then he felt guilty - realizing suddenly that this oasis lounge felt out of place and unreal given the people jostling for space and buying food out of coolers outside. The ride was rocky and he felt seasick by the time they got across to the Kissy terminal an hour later. He felt sick to his core, trying to imagine the experience of those that rode in ships on these waters for a much longer journey to slavery. He did not even realize his wallet had been stolen in the hustle and bustle of the ferry until later. Luckily, he had taken Baindu's advise not to keep all his money together and the wallet that was taken had only a few hundred dollars in it and no cards.

The drive from Kissy to Spur loop was its own adventure. Horns blaring, hawkers jostling up to the car window every time they were stopped and drivers dashing in and out of traffic and around potholes. Baindu laughed when Shawn asked for the road signs. The city looked like it was happening the same way the airport was - in what looked like mass confusion, yet everyone was getting ahead and cars weren't hitting people. Shawn felt like he was being re-educated. He could tell when they left the East-end of the city into the West-end. There were more barred houses prominently perched between the tin shacks that were scattered everywhere.

He'd been overwhelmed with her parent's welcome and the comfort of their air-conditioned home. He questioned the amount of house help they had - didn't that feel wrong? No, Baindu had said, what other employment would they get otherwise? He'd been relieved at how well the help were treated when Baindu gave him a tour of their quarters. He couldn't live with being served by them otherwise. He learned how many children of Baindu's family staff were being educated as a benefit of their employment. He found out how much Baindu's parents did to serve their communities in ways Baindu had never mentioned.

The weeks before the wedding were a whirlwind. Baindu, Shawn and his aunts that arrived after him got fitted and had their traditional outfits tailor-made. They went to the beaches in and around Freetown and drove around the peninsula. They went to

Baindu's family village in the South. Shawn remarked that it was funny that he felt less conflicted and more familiar with the village setting and had enjoyed eating with his hands, watching the children play and the women carry buckets on their heads topless, with their African print wraps around their waists. He was appalled and ashamed to realize how much he'd been conditioned to think by popular media that this is what Africa really looks like. And how the media conveyed only the hardship and very little of the joy, curiosity and hospitality of the people he was meeting. Baindu had said to him: "All of what you're experiencing are real African experiences - It's all real, the good, the bad and the ugly."

Shawn and his aunts were assigned an interpreter and a wedding planner to help them collect all the items they needed for the traditional wedding ceremony to show their respects when they came to ask for Baindu's hand. They were taught about the calabash that they needed to bring to do so. The calabash was a medium-sized wooden traditional mixing bowl that needed to be filled with symbolic items significant for marriage. These were items like kolanuts, a bitter-sweet nut that was historically used to show welcome and hospitality and signify the nature of marriage. Likewise, needles and thread, to imply marriage must constantly be mended when rifts occur. There was traditional fabric as gifts for the bride and her family and several other items, including the dowry or bride price.

Shawn struggled with the dowry. He told Baindu he could not partake in a practice that indicated he was paying for her. Baindu had looked at him piercingly and said: "you could never pay for me. The dowry is completely symbolic at this point, a token. However, to not include it would be to insult my family. They will not accept the calabash when they check for all the items which must be included, which means they will not accept the marriage. We could just go be married by the Justice of the Peace instead and be done with it, but that will mean there'll be some elders in my family who will never consider us married. So, you choose."

After talking to Baindu's dad and confirming these views, Shawn had chosen to go ahead with it. He'd been reassured when Baindu's dad had laughed and told him that in their family they had resolved the abuses and controversies of the dowry system by simply giving the cash amount or in-kind item, which was traditionally gold, back to the bride. The dowry was traditionally meant for her financial security in case of divorce anyway. In the past, families were supposed to keep the amount or item in trust for the bride, Dad had explained. But of course, some families often used it for themselves and had been motivated to marry off women based on how much the families could get in dowry. This was not always ill-intended, he'd said. Sometimes these things had happened because of poverty or necessity even though it of course put women at risk. The issues were well-understood now and dowry had become mostly a symbolic token. Shawn and Baindu would often laugh afterwards, that the 'cheque' included for her dowry which was handed back to Baindu, was from their joint Canadian account.

The traditional wedding happened on the day before the church ceremony, followed by the bachelor eve party in the evening. Shawn had loved the ceremony after all. It was as much a ritual of the meeting and joining of their two families as it was of him asking for and receiving his bride's hand. His family had been prepped to expect the parade of false brides that were brought out before Baindu came out to accept his betroth. The parade of the biblical Leahs for his Rachel were all Baindu's beautiful sisters and cousins and they had to be 'encouraged' to leave – which meant giving them token amounts of cash until they were satisfied enough to go and get the real bride in their stead. It became a pretty hilarious bargaining and cajoling process depending on how obstinate the false brides were.

Shawn was well prepared with appeasing words that softened the women and after only four false brides, out came Baindu, dressed in a cream lace traditional gown with the older women dancing and singing around her. She was breathtaking. She accepted the calabash and after the women confirmed it was complete, Baindu and Shawn were literally joined with their hands held and wrapped together as they vowed their love. Shawn had never experienced so much love, hustle, food and color in a room before. He and his aunts marveled at the ashobi-clad men and women, who were family and friends wearing the same print fabric chosen for the wedding and who were serving, dancing and celebrating throughout the ceremony and the party that followed.

That night, Baindu's dad said to him: "Son, I know you will love and respect my daughter. I have asked her if you two decided to do this for the papers and she said no. I hope she is telling me the truth, because I want you to consider coming home after her studies. You don't need to stay abroad if you don't want to - please consider coming home."

~~~

♪ ♪ *We Yawoo fine oh!* ♪ ♪

♪ ♪ *We Yawoo fine oh!* ♪ ♪

"Well, time to go, Shawn," Baindu said with a glint in her eye, nuzzling close to him. It was the end of the night after the wedding reception and party. They had changed into their newly-wed ashobi outfits which was a signal that they were ready to leave. When they came out, the DJ had stopped the party music and prompted the final round of goombay dancing for the family and guests to see them off.

"That is, unless you prefer to stay longer and not…consummate this marriage yet!" Baindu continued, chuckling.

Shawn's eyes went ablaze with passion.

Without a word, he scooped her up in his arms and started
~~~

dancing his way toward their borrowed luxury getaway car. One of Baindu's dad's diplomat friends had loaned it to them. Shawn was still dumbfounded that he'd be riding his first Range Rover in Freetown, Sierra Leone, of all places.

♪ ♪ *All dem bella dem sidom na we dey go so mama ya!* ♪ ♪

♪ ♪ *All dem bella dem sidom na we dey go so mama ya!* ♪ ♪

The crowd went wild, cheering, clapping and dancing along with Shawn as he made his way. Baindu's brothers and cousins joined him and hoisted Baindu way up in the air. Dollar and Leone bills came raining in their direction. Shawn saw the house-help's son nimbly ruffling through the crowd and collecting bills from between people's legs as they fell. He felt the rain of sweat and spittle mixed with an unbridled joy and celebration like he'd never experienced before wash over him.

♪ ♪ *All dem bella dem sidom na we dey go so mama ya!* ♪ ♪

♪ ♪ *All dem bella dem sidom na we dey go so mama ya!* ♪ ♪

They finally made it to the car and the men helped Shawn retrieve his bride from the air and deposit her safely, albeit not tremendously gently, into the car. She collapsed against him, laughing joyously. The driver set the car in gear, moving slowly forward through the crowd. Shawn pulled Baindu against him, kissing her slowly, deeply, passionately, as people started parting away from the car, while still dancing. The youngest men and boys started running alongside the car as one yelled out:

"E yeah, dem day kiss, dem day kiss!!" *Look, they are kissing, they are kissing!*

Shawn felt Baindu chuckle against his lips as the kids kept yelling, "dem day kiss!" The car finally moved into full speed ahead. And off they went, Tokeh Beach bound for their honeymoon. The side runners were left trailing behind the car, still running, waving and dancing. It was time for Shawn and Baindu to begin working out their happily ever after, holding with them the full history of their ancestors from these African shores to Britain and the Americas, to Nova Scotia and all the way back.

From slavery to freedom.

From bondage to revolution.

From poverty to wealth.

From servitude to service.

From hatred to love.

Lonta. Na De Wod Dat. The End. Word!

ABOUT THE AUTHOR

Yabome was born in Germany, grew up in Sierra Leone, West Africa, and completed her undergraduate and graduate studies in Canada and the United States. She is a social scientist, writer, facilitator and curator of African identity and leadership stories. Yabome holds a doctorate in Human and Organization Development. She works, teaches, speaks, does research and writes in the field of Leadership and Organizational Change/Development and Social Change, especially related to Africa. See www.sldconsulting.org for more information or contact Yabome directly at yabome@sldconsulting.org.

NOTE FROM YABOME ON WHY THIS PROJECT

I was sitting at a conference listening absent-mindedly to the distant voice of a speaker. I was wearing the look of studious attention I had perfected in the midst of boredom, nodding and smiling appropriately by rote while my mind races along engaging and entertaining itself. Almost suddenly, but simultaneously like what felt like slow motion, the speaker's voice went from distant to present for me when she said "Fred Allen [American Radio Comedian] once said '***A human being is nothing but a story with skin around it.***'"

You see I love stories and love anything that reminds me how much stories connects us to our individual and common humanity. I believe also that we are *more than* ***a*** *story*. And in our increasingly complex world, Chimamanda Ngozi Adichie's could not have better articulated *the danger of a single story* in her 2009 Ted Talk.

I believe we are a web of stories. A web informed by strands that go back to our ancestry and heritage, and that grows and shifts in every interaction we have. I believe that telling the stories of our lives makes us more fully whole, uncovering richer understandings of each strand and shaping and reshaping each of our webs to make them fuller – beautifully prepared to catch what is meant to nourish us, withstand what threatens to break us and when we break, rebuild our webs to be even stronger than before. And when our being and becoming ends with our last breath on this side of eternity, the web of our life will continue through the strands we leave behind with those we loved, those we touched and even those we never knew.

So, I write, because I agree with these scholars who handed me a strand from the web of their lives when I read their words:

- "what is most personal is most general" (Carl Rogers).
- "it is the job of good sociology to reveal the public issues inherent in troubles personally felt" (C. Wright Mills).
- "identifying possible inconsistencies and inner contradictions is a powerful way to examine our own inconsistencies and inner contradictions" (Chris Argyris).

I write fiction, informed by my own lived experiences, about my humanity, my womanity and my identities. I write, because there is an abundance of stories that keep welling up through me, itching to be told. So, I finally gave in to the common stories that beat in my heart and form in my mind from everyday moments – a casual conversation, a stirring from the beauty of nature around me, an awkward moment at work.

I hope that the web of these stories connects somewhere with yours and if it doesn't, that it brings to focus an understanding of a part of the larger web of life that we are all creating and part of together.

Yabome.

CPSIA information can be obtained
at www.ICGtesting.com
Printed in the USA
LVHW111729170920
666361LV00006B/982